WITCHING FOR LOVE ON VALENTINE'S DAY

A WESTWICK WITCHES PARANORMAL MYSTERY

COLLEEN CROSS

ALSO BY COLLEEN CROSS

Westwick Witches Cozy Mysteries

Witch You Well

Rags to Witches

Witch and Famous

Christmas Witch List

Witching Hour Dead

Witching for Love on Valentines Day

Katerina Carter Fraud Legal Thrillers

Exit Strategy

Game Theory

Blowout

Greenwash

Red Handed

Blue Moon

Nonfiction

Anatomy of a Ponzi Scheme

WITCHING FOR LOVE ON VALENTINE'S DAY

Til death do us part...

Cendrine West and the Westwick witches look forward to an enchanting Valentine's Day full of romance, secret admirers, and maybe even a marriage proposal or two. Love is in the air but Aunt Pearl doesn't care.

Ruby's latest business venture brings unexpected guests and a mystery proposal sends Cen on a quest. Then Cupid's arrow catches a curse, and suddenly all hell breaks loose!

CHAPTER 1

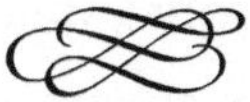

I come from a long line of accomplished witches. People think witches have all sorts of methods at their disposal to earn a nice living, but it's simply not true. We follow a strict set of rules prohibiting the use of witchcraft for financial or material gain. Westwick Corners is a small town with very few jobs, so we needed ingenuity and creativity to make ends meet.

The West family's primary source of income is our Westwick Corners Inn, our boutique bed and breakfast, which keeps us afloat financially. In addition to multiple roles at the inn, I am also the publisher and sole employee of the Westwick Corners Weekly. I acquired the community newspaper from the retiring owner a few years ago, buying myself a job in the process. At the moment though, I was completely focused on my growling stomach that demanded to be fed.

The aroma of freshly baked banana muffins wafted

toward me as I pushed open the large door that separated our guest dining room from the kitchen. Entering the kitchen was a definite no-no for my diet. I was calorie watching and had met my daily muffin quota with a cranberry muffin at breakfast an hour ago. Mom's daily baking was a constant occupational hazard. Regardless, I entered the kitchen with fresh resolve, determined not to let even a morsel of Mom's baking pass through my lips.

Mom opened the door of the large industrial stainless-steel oven with oversized oven mitts. She pulled out a heavy cast iron pan and held it out for me. "A muffin for your thoughts, Cen?"

My mouth watered but I shook my head. "I can't even zip up the dress I bought especially for Valentine's Day. I need to lose five more pounds by tonight and another five pounds before dinnertime tomorrow." My stomach growled in protest.

Mom laughed and placed the muffin tin on a trivet on the counter to cool beside a second batch of blueberry muffins. "Five pounds is doable in a week or two, not a day. You can't starve yourself, and you shouldn't. You look lovely just the way you are."

Easy for Mom to say—she had been an athlete in her younger days, a star sprinter on the college track and field team. Nowadays, she burned calories managing the inn and tending the large vegetable garden that provided most of the inn's food. Unlike me, she was disciplined and fit in a workout most days. She ate whatever she wanted and didn't gain an ounce.

Aunt Pearl did none of those things, but she effortlessly maintained her bony ninety-pound bodyweight. The West gene pool had somehow bypassed me. I packed on the pounds just by writing out my grocery list. I was fuller, taller, and fairer than any of my relatives. Even my straight blonde locks stood out from the family standard of brunette curls. Mom had always been vague about our family genealogy. If it weren't for my spellcasting abilities, I would have thought I had been adopted.

The kitchen door swung open so hard that it banged against the wall.

"Geez, Ruby, what are you burning now?" Aunt Pearl scowled as she entered the kitchen. The age gap between Mom, the youngest, and Aunt Pearl, the oldest, was over a dozen years but you'd never know it. Aunt Pearl looked exceptionally young for her age due to her active running from the law lifestyle.

When she wasn't busy flouting laws or setting things on fire, she harassed the town sheriff for kicks. She was a one-woman crime wave and the most rebellious senior citizen you could ever imagine.

Mom waved a hand in dismissal. "I was just encouraging Cen to try a muffin. I've got blueberry, banana, and chocolate chip. Want one?"

Aunt Pearl's eyes narrowed, primed for an argument. "Baking is a waste of time. Go buy the stuff. If you both spent more time casting spells instead of playing with cast iron pans, this world—and our town—would be a better place."

Mom shook her head. "Baking is cheaper and healthier than anything you get at the grocery store. The inn puts food on the table. Last I checked, Pearl's Charm School was closed due to low enrolment. Even Cen's newspaper makes money." Mom glanced at me, her expression doubtful.

I crossed my arms defensively. "Of course, my newspaper makes money. I've already sold a month's worth of advertising for my special Valentine's Day edition." My family thought of my community newspaper as a hobby and it frustrated me to no end.

"No need to get angry, Cen. I was just making a point," Mom said.

"I wasn't get—"

Aunt Pearl snorted. "Cen's just mad because nobody reads her articles, Ruby. You know as well as I do that people buy it only for the flyers and coupons."

Aunt Pearl's day job was the inn's housekeeper, but she also operated Pearl's Charm School, a school for witches. Her students never lasted more than a semester, driven away by her cantankerous temperament. But the slightest criticism of Aunt Pearl's school sent her into such a tizzy that Mom and I generally kept our mouths shut. Who was she to doubt my business acumen?

The inn, and our town, prospered whenever tourists came to town. The trick was attracting them to our hidden little hamlet that was off the beaten track. We had a few lean years at the beginning, but Mom's idea of turning our family mansion into a boutique bed and breakfast several years ago had been a great success. We had recently added a bar and estate winery on our property and marketed our inn as a cozy little getaway from the hustle and bustle of city life.

Despite our modest success, it was a constant battle to get Aunt Pearl to do her share of the work. Aunt Pearl hated the very idea of visitors. She devoted as much energy to driving away visitors as we did to attracting them. Our very existence depended on tourism, but Aunt Pearl couldn't accept that.

Aunt Pearl walked over to the counter and tore off a piece of freshly baked banana muffin. She popped the morsel into her mouth and grimaced. "This is terrible, Ruby! You can't serve this crap to our guests."

"You don't even like banana muffins. Why did you take one?" Mom wiped her forehead with the back of her hand and sighed.

"Doesn't matter. Nobody's going to eat this garbage." Aunt Pearl raised her hand to her mouth and spit the muffin morsel into her palm. She walked over to the garbage and brushed the crumbs off her palm and into the garbage.

I scowled. "You wasted that muffin on purpose."

Aunt Pearl sniffed. "Too sweet for my liking."

"Our guests love my baking, even if you don't," Mom said. "Not that you care. You barely clean the rooms anymore, and that new bartender you hired is terrible. He over-pours and under-serves."

Aunt Pearl rolled her eyes. "The customers love Lucky. I told you, Ruby, I can't spend any more time in this tourist trap. I've got to manage Pearl's Charm School."

Mom sighed. "The inn is your business too, Pearl. You've got to do something about Lucky. He's costing us all our profits."

"You could bartend again, Aunt Pearl. That would save us some money." People were more accepting of a cranky bartender than a cranky housekeeper. Alcohol seemed to smooth the tension.

"Nope. Too busy." Aunt Pearl shook her head. "Why don't you do it?"

I shook my head. "I already check in the guests, keep the books, and do all the laundry. I can't possibly do more. Besides, you don't even have any students right now."

"That's just temporary while I update the curriculum." Aunt Pearl's eyes narrowed as she studied me. "You know, Cen, I could use some spell beta testers. You help me, I help you. You could use a few spell refreshers yourself."

"Stop changing the subject, Aunt Pearl. My spellcasting is just fine." My witchcraft could use a little polish, but I practised regularly with what little spare time I had. Mom was right, though. The inn was our number one priority. It fed us, clothed us, and kept a roof over our heads. Witchcraft was a nice extra, but it didn't pay the bills.

Mom stood at the sink, washing and rinsing dishes. "Pearl, if business doesn't pick up soon, you'll have to get rid of Lucky. We can't afford his wages."

"You can't do that," Aunt Pearl protested. "I promised his mom that I'd give him a job."

"You shouldn't make commitments without asking me first," Mom said. "Lucky doesn't even show up half the time. When he does, he's late. If it was up to me, I would have let him go after his first day on the job. It's almost like you want our business to fail."

Aunt Pearl pouted. "Lucky is a fantastic bartender. He makes amazing drinks. He's perfect for the job."

"Only if money's no object," I said. "Every drink he mixes is a double. I doubt that Lucky is even his real name." Aunt Pearl had hired Lucky three weeks ago without any resume or references when he moved to town. He was a man with no past that had seemingly arrived out of nowhere. We knew nothing about him, and he knew next to nothing about bartending. He would bankrupt us if we weren't careful.

Mom sighed. "He dresses like a gangster. I know you can't judge people by their appearances but why does he need those flashy suits? Why does he have to change clothes two or three times in a single shift? He's always arriving late and leaving early. Face it, Pearl, he's not employee material. He's got other things on his mind besides tending bar."

"Okay, okay. I'll talk to him. In the meantime, just cut him some slack. Everybody deserves a second chance." Aunt Pearl helped herself to another muffin, a blueberry one this time. She tore off a chunk of muffin and held it between her fingers. She held it up to her nose and sniffed it. She dropped it on the counter with a grimace. "Well, maybe not everyone."

I frowned. "Mom spends a lot of time baking everything fresh for our guests. Now, because of you, she needs to bake another batch."

Aunt Pearl crossed her arms in defiance. A smug smile spread across her face as she looked at the muffin on the counter and then me. "If the muffins are so great, Cen, why aren't you having any?"

"I'm on a diet." I looked longingly at what was left of the muffin. Blueberry was my second favorite after banana. Aunt Pearl was purposely taunting me, and I felt my resolve waver.

"You're going to let it go to waste?" Aunt Pearl grinned mischievously.

I gave in and reached for the muffin. I broke off a piece and tasted it. "Yum…it's delicious, Mom."

Mom smiled and then turned back toward the oven. She removed yet another muffin pan from the oven and placed it on the stovetop to cool.

Mom oversaw the inn's daily operations. She also prepared breakfast, lunch, and dinner and baked delicious treats daily. Aunt Pearl only had to clean eight guestrooms, most of which were only occupied on weekends. Yet she did her level best to create a poor guest experience in her own sly way. While the rooms always had fresh linens and toiletries, guests often awoke to strange noises at night, windows that suddenly opened or closed, and other mysterious shenanigans. She was literally haunting our guests. Sometimes they were spooked enough to check out early.

Aunt Pearl always blamed Grandma Vi. My ghostly grandmother passed away several years ago but had never left her beloved home. Our resident ghost was a benign spirit who mostly kept to herself. She simply enjoyed our company and the cozy ambience of the inn. She would never drive away our paying guests.

Aunt Pearl's spells and shenanigans hurt business, which was exactly her intention.

Which brings me to yet another of my inn duties: cleaning up my aunt's messes with secret counter-spells of my own. That job I didn't mind so much since it had a side benefit of further honing my witchcraft. I was now a better witch than Aunt Pearl, though she would never admit it.

I kept tabs on Aunt Pearl's whereabouts and deescalated any run-ins with the town's law enforcement. They happened often, and our sheriffs came and went with astonishing frequency. Until the latest sheriff, that is. The one positive thing to come of Aunt Pearl's law-breaking was that it had introduced me to my wonderful sheriff boyfriend, Tyler Gates.

The thought of Tyler's warm brown eyes and infectious smile made my heart melt. Maybe he'd be more than just a boyfriend soon, maybe even as soon as tomorrow night. We had Valentine's Day dinner reservations at the fanciest restaurant in nearby Shady Creek. We'd talked about marriage casually before, but lately Tyler had been dropping hints.

When that unmentionable thing that was about to happen, actually happened, I wanted to be dressed for the occasion, wearing my sparkly new red Valentine's Day dress. I would look spectacular when I accepted his proposal, even if I had to squeeze my chubby self into my slightly too-small dress. I had to basically starve myself between now and then, but I was up for it. All that wouldn't be ruined with a calorie-dense muffin.

I glanced down and gasped. All that was left in my hand were crumbs. I had eaten an entire muffin without even realizing!

Aunt Pearl eyed Mom suspiciously. "Who exactly are you baking for, Ruby? Our last guests checked out yesterday morning."

I had wondered too, because I wasn't aware of any reservations at the inn. That was also odd. We were usually fully booked for Valentine's Day weekend.

Mom's face flushed as she placed a large wicker basket lined with a linen napkin onto the countertop. She lifted one of the muffin pans and carefully flipped it over. The muffins tumbled into the basket and the aroma of baked banana wafted through the air. "I, uh… can't talk now. I've got more cooking and baking to finish."

I salivated at the aroma as my stomach growled for more. "Who did you say—?"

Mom didn't answer.

Grandma Vi's transparent form suddenly materialized. She floated through the wall that separated the kitchen from the dining room. My ghostly grandma was still very much part of our daily life. Thankfully, she could be seen only by family members.

She hovered across from me and said in a sing-song voice, "Mmm…muffffffins! Your favorites, Cen!"

I shook my head no. "I'm on a diet, remember?"

Grandma Vi snorted. "You've blown the diet, Cen. In fact, you're looking rather plump lately."

"You think I'm fat?" My shoulders slumped in defeat. What had possessed me to buy a dress two sizes too small? Dumb, dumb, dumb. Losing a few pounds a month had sounded easy enough last fall when I still had months to achieve my goal. But Valentines' Day was tomorrow. Instead of losing weight, I had even gained a few more pounds over Christmas. I had helped myself a little too much to Mom's holiday baking and our family's newly launched line of Witching Hour estate wines. In the meantime, Valentine's Day had drawn closer and closer, and now it was tomorrow.

Grandma Vi hovered in front of me, her transparent body a barrier of sorts between me and the counter. "Just telling you the honest truth, Cen. Even if you starve yourself, there's no way that dress will fit you by tomorrow."

Aunt Pearl snorted. "Cast a spell, Cen. Upsize that silly dress."

I crossed my arms. "You know I can't do that. That's an abuse of power and against WICCA rules." Frivolous use of magic was frowned upon by the Witches International Community Craft Association. Fitting into the dress was important, but not WICCA-ban level important.

Aunt Pearl rolled her eyes. "You're so ridiculous. Just bend the rules a little. Nobody's ever going to know."

That was a lie. If I broke any rule, no matter how slight, Aunt Pearl would tattle to Aunt Amber, who was a top WICCA executive. Aunt Amber would insist on holding up her rule-breaking niece as an example to the entire WICCA membership. I would be publicly humiliated in front of the whole witch community. Not a chance I was willing to take.

I was mad at myself more than anything. I'd had plenty of time to lose the weight and I had blown it. My time was up.

Unless I lost something like a pound an hour, it simply wasn't going to happen.

I flashed back to the gorgeous red dress that hung in my closet, a sleeveless red silk number with a mid-calf hem that hugged my curves in all the right places. At least it had when I had tried it on before Christmas with the back zipper undone. I hadn't been able to zip it up then, and now it was even tighter. In fact, it barely slid over my hips. The dress was one of those timeless pieces that would look fashionable in any decade. The round neckline was adorned with tiny handsewn crystal beads that reflected the light and complemented my fair complexion.

My impulse purchase at Bunny's Key to Fashion, Westwick Corners' only women's clothing store, had been a mistake. I now realized that Bunny's compliments were simply a ploy to move her inventory. I couldn't possibly look incredibly gorgeous in a dress that I couldn't even zip up. Bunny lied. But like it or not, the dress was now mine. It was also the only proposal-worthy dress I owned, and I was dead-set on wearing it. For that to happen, I needed either magical alterations or a non-magical backup plan.

Grandma Vi broke into my thoughts. "Cen! Any special news to share?"

"Nope." I stared at the floor. hoping that Mom and Aunt Pearl didn't pick up on Grandma Vi's hint. Her mindreading abilities were annoying at the best of times, and I really resented her intruding into my secret thoughts. I would reveal my life-changing news after tomorrow night, when Tyler proposed.

I couldn't imagine spending my life with anyone else. Tyler and I were made for each other, and for me at least, it had been love at first sight. An added bonus was that Tyler completely accepted my wacky family, even if Aunt Pearl considered him her sworn enemy.

Mom covered the muffin basket with a tea towel and carried it to the back door. She slipped her feet into clogs and reached for the door handle.

Grandma Vi floated in front of Mom, blocking her path. She pointed in the opposite direction. "The dining room is that way, Ruby. Where are you going with those muffins?"

Mom cleared her throat and looked around nervously. "I'm, uh…taking them to the Rocklin Mansion."

Grandma Vi gasped. "Why? That place is abandoned. Nobody's lived there for decades."

Mom sucked in her breath. "Well, that's about to change."

"Did someone buy the place?" The Rocklin Mansion had sat empty for as long as I could remember, long before our real estate market had collapsed for good. Rumors had circulated for years that it was haunted, and most people in town went out of their way to avoid the place. Whether it was or wasn't haunted, new arrivals in town was always big news, so why was Mom so secretive?

Mom's hand tightened on the door handle, but she didn't say a word. She didn't have to. Her eyes were downcast, like she had been caught in a lie.

Grandma Vi's aura turned a dark crimson, a sure sign she was angry. "Why would anyone want to stay there?"

Mom glanced down at her watch. "Come with me, Cen. I'll explain everything once we're there."

Aunt Pearl's eyes narrowed. "Explain what, Ruby? You know that place is cursed."

Mom opened the door a crack. "I'm running late. Cen, are you coming?"

"I can't, Mom. I have to get out the Valentine's Day edition of the newspaper." I had a couple of last-minute tasks before I published the special issue. It was chock-full of romance, recipes, and secret valentines.

This year there were twice as many valentine messages as last year, making it one of my most profitable editions. There were messages from secret admirers, current and wannabe girlfriends and boyfriends, and the cutest of all, a full page spread of valentines drawn by kids at the local elementary school. But one very special valentine stood out above the others. An anonymous person—I suspected it was a man—had taken out a full-page advertisement for his as yet unnamed secret sweetheart.

His wasn't the only anonymous valentine's wish. There were plenty of others, and people enjoyed guessing who the senders and the recipients were. But I always knew who paid for the ads. Except for the buyer of this year's full-page ad, who remained a mystery to me. The only clues were an envelope slipped under my office door with the Valentine's day wish and a very generous cash payment enclosed.

Too generous, in fact. The money was enough to cover my expenses for the entire month and part of the next. While I was grateful to be in the black for another few months, I worried that my anonymous customer had mistakenly overpaid, and I wanted to make things right. More than anything though, I really wanted to know who this sweet, romantic well-wisher was.

The wish was sentimental but too general to guess who the sender was, and my curiosity was piqued.

Aunt Pearl snorted. "Nobody reads your paper, Cen. Stop wasting your time."

"You're wrong. You'd be surprised at how popular my newspaper actually is." I was tired of Aunt Pearl's constant putdowns. One of the valentine's messages came from Aunt Pearl's boyfriend, Earl. I couldn't wait to see the look on her face when I proved her wrong.

"The only surprise is how long you've kept that money-losing rag solvent. Waste of time and money if you ask me."

"Well, nobody asked you, and you won't want to miss my Valentine's Day issue." As much as I loved my aunt, I couldn't fathom what that sweet man saw in her. He was polite, laid-back, and kind to everyone. In other words, Earl was Aunt Pearl's polar opposite.

"Not gonna happen, Cen." Aunt Pearl dismissed me with a hand wave. "I don't have time for that sentimental nonsense."

I'd spent extra hours this week rereading all the valentine messages, not because I had to, but simply because they made me smile. There really is an abundance of love in this world. It swirls all around us, invisible unless we listen and look for it. Bad luck, bad moods, and misunderstandings are just temporary roadblocks. But too often, we don't push through the barriers and love is lost. I truly believe that kindness and goodness wins, as long as we allow it in. The valentine messages only reaffirmed my belief.

Most people are good at heart, but some need a nudge, even a shove, to express their love. There's nothing like a valentine's wish to get your heart back on track. I imagined many smiling faces tomorrow, as people sipped their morning coffees and discovered the one special valentine message meant especially for them. Sometimes life was crappy, but love always got you through. As long as you let it, that is.

"Okay, Mom, let's go." Arguing with Aunt Pearl was pointless, and I had no time to spare. It conveniently delayed my dress try-on a little longer and delayed my dread at what I knew was true. My dress wasn't going to fit no matter what I did.

"Good, because we're already late." Mom ushered me through the back door.

We walked around to the front of the property just in time to see Lucky slide out of the passenger seat of his rusty, dented green Ford pickup truck. He staggered a few steps before he stopped and stared at us. His hair was tousled as if he had just woken up. He was dressed formally in a tux that was disheveled and slept in. His jacket was unbuttoned, and his shirt was untucked.

"Hello, ladies." He saluted us and stumbled forward toward the Witching Post Bar and Grill at the opposite end of the parking lot.

"That man's got to go," Mom muttered as she waved half-heartedly.

"He's already drunk," I whispered. "He should not be driving."

Mom sighed. "We can't go on like this. One of these days—"

"Happy hour at noon—don't forget!" Lucky swayed on his feet as he pointed a finger at us. "Did you say something?"

"Nope," I said.

He nodded and continued on his trek across the parking lot until he reached the bar's front entrance. He turned the handle without using his key first. He turned and waved before heading inside.

An unlocked bar with booze, free for the taking, was a sure way to bankruptcy. Lucky was a liability and Mom was right about something else too. We needed new ways to make money, even if Aunt Pearl and Grandma Vi disagreed. How the Rocklin mansion factored into Mom's plans was a mystery. I had no idea why Grandma Vi and Aunt Pearl were so opposed to our visit, but I was about to find out.

CHAPTER 2

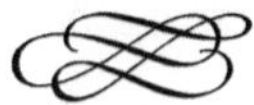

$\mathcal{I}$t was a cold, crisp, February morning and the low clouds threatened snow. I leaned back in the Subaru's front passenger seat, thankful that Mom had turned the heat up full blast. The warm air cleared a wide arc across the frosty glass as the windshield slowly defrosted.

Inside the car, the mood was far from warm and cozy.

"What do you mean, you rented out the Rocklin Mansion?" I asked. "I know we need the money, but you can't just rent out a house that doesn't belong to you. That's trespassing. It's also illegal."

Mom shook her head. "It's perfectly fine. Nobody's lived there for years. I'll leave it better than I found it, and nobody will be the wiser."

"You're basically stealing, Mom. If you don't have permission from the owners—"

Mom interrupted me. "Possession is 9/10th of the law, Cen."

"No, it isn't. How can we manage another property, Mom? Aunt Pearl isn't doing her share at the inn anymore, and Lucky costs us more money than he brings in."

"It will all work out, don't worry," Mom said brightly. It was a quiet Saturday morning as we drove through downtown Westwick Corners, and the stores in town were still closed. The streets were mostly deserted, with few signs of cars or people. I spotted Tyler's jeep parked outside City Hall. He was a morning person and liked to get an early start. Our town didn't have much crime, but Tyler, as the town's sole law enforcement, always had something to do.

I didn't want to add even more to his already long list of police duties, all because of Mom's hairbrained—and illegal —scheme.

My mind wandered to our Valentine's Day date tomorrow. I'd be in my red silk dress and Tyler in a suit, his hand on mine as we gazed at each other across a candlelit table at our favorite restaurant. His promise of something special kept me wondering and hoping. We had talked marriage. Could it really be an engagement ring? I was excited and nervous at the same time. Our lives were about to change, and I couldn't wait.

We passed Molly's Café and Bistro on the right, where a few vehicles, mostly pickup trucks were parked out front. The warm golden light from the restaurant's cozy interior spilled out onto the frost-covered landscape outside. I turned sideways in my seat to see if anyone I knew was inside, but it was impossible to tell.

Mom shifted her gaze from the road ahead to me. "Our

new guests called out of the blue. I couldn't turn them away and the inn wasn't big enough. With no other accommodations for miles around I had to come up with an alternative plan. That's how I got the Rocklin mansion."

I frowned. "You managed to contact the Rocklins after all these years?" The Rocklins were the town's 'other' witch family. At least they had been, until they had left town in a hurry under mysterious and unexplained circumstances. It happened years before I was born, and the mansion had stood empty and derelict ever since, unlived in and unloved.

Silence.

"Why that place, Mom? There's good reason that place is abandoned. It's a dump."

"I needed somewhere spacious, and that place is big and was just sitting empty. Since it's been abandoned for years, no one will care if I take it over for a week. It was beautiful once, and I've restored it to its former glory. In fact, it's better than ever. Everyone wins." Mom locked her eyes on the road ahead.

It was so unlike Mom to break the law or violate someone's property rights. Yet here she was, basically commandeering someone else's property to rent to strangers. All in the name of profit. Her actions were completely uncharacteristic. Part of me wanted to say nothing and stay out of trouble, but as a West, I was already guilty by association.

"You can't take over someone's private property, Mom. I can't manage any more responsibilities either." Between my newspaper and my multiple jobs at the inn, I was at my breaking point.

Mom's creeping takeover would start small. One week would turn into two, and two weeks into a month, illegally occupying a property that didn't belong to her. Aunt Pearl wasn't the only lawbreaker in the family. Once Tyler found out, he might reconsider whether or not he, as a sheriff, wanted to marry into a family of criminals.

As I stewed in my seat, I caught a flash of movement in the rear-view mirror.

Mom must have seen it too, because she glanced in the rear-view mirror. "I couldn't find the owner, but my renovations are payment enough."

A voice hissed from the backseat. "Undo it, Ruby!"

I was too afraid to turn around and confront our carjacker. Instead, I shrieked. "Don't hurt us!"

Mom swerved sharply onto the road's shoulder. The car tilted and veered off the pavement, tilting crazily and almost flipping. Mom regained control just in time and steered back onto the asphalt. The car's suspension thudded as it regained traction on the pavement.

"You're over the top dramatic, Cen. Relax." Grandma Vi floated between us and hovered over the center console. "You better not go through with this, Ruby."

"You scared us half to death, Grandma. Mom could have hit someone."

Mom glared at me. "Don't be ridiculous! I'm an excellent driver."

Grandma Vi shook her head. "You almost got us killed! Good thing no one else is on the road this early."

I didn't point out the fact that Grandma Vi was a ghost and therefore already dead.

"Stop being a backseat driver or I'll pull over and I'll...I'll—"

"You'll do what, Ruby? Make me get out and walk?"

Grandma Vi laughed. "Ghosts don't walk. You can't make me do anything. The Rocklin curse is serious business. We break that promise and there will be hell to pay."

"What curse?" Breaking and entering was bad enough, but a curse? I couldn't handle any more bad news.

Grandma Vi's mouth dropped open. "You never told Cen?"

"Told me what?" My gaze shifted from Grandma Vi in the backseat to Mom.

Mom stared straight ahead instead of meeting my gaze. "You don't believe in silly curses, do you, Cen?"

"Of course, I believe in curses, Mom! A curse by any other name is a malevolent, long-lasting spell, right? Basically, it's evil witchcraft."

"Well, technically yes, but this whole curse thing is nonsense. Why is it that whenever I find a way to earn our family a living, everybody criticizes?"

I hadn't meant to hurt her feelings. "I'm not, Mom. I'm just kind of—"

"Kind of what—worried? You constantly worry about things that never happen, Cen." Mom stared at the road ahead and blinked back tears. She drove faster.

"Slow down, Mom. What's this curse all about?" Trespassing was one thing. A genuine curse was quite another.

"It's no big deal," Mom said.

"Tell Cen the truth, Ruby," Grandma Vi cried. "Your greedy actions have triggered a curse that harms all of us."

Mom glared at Grandma Vi through the rear-view mirror. "Is putting a roof over our heads greed? Is having money to eat greed? I don't see anybody else contributing to our expenses."

"Eyes on the road, Ruby," Grandma Vi said curtly.

Mom scowled and gunned the gas pedal.

My head slammed back into the headrest from the g-force.

"What happens to us if the curse gets activated?" I imagined the worst. Would we be harmed, or even killed? Would the Rocklins return to avenge us? Would the town burn down to ashes?

Mom sighed. "We'll talk about it later."

Grandma Vi groaned from the backseat. Whether she disagreed with Mom's comment, driving, or both, wasn't clear.

I stared out the passenger window, silently sick with dread. I didn't like arguing with Mom, but she wasn't making any sense.

Mom glanced over and said reassuringly, "It's been decades, Cen. If the curse actually existed, something would have happened by now."

Grandma Vi sighed in the backseat. "The curse is reactivated, thanks to you. We just don't know it yet."

I turned around in my seat. "You owe me an explanation. How can I protect myself if I don't know what the curse is about?"

"Don't worry about it. I've got everything taken care of." Mom's voice was curt. Her knuckles whitened as her fingers gripped the steering wheel even tighter.

Grandma Vi let out a heavy sigh. "Cen deserves to know about the curse, Ruby. After all, she's a target."

CHAPTER 3

"Why does the curse impact me? I haven't done anything to deserve it." If I was the target of a supernatural hit, I needed protection. How could I protect myself from something I knew nothing about?

Grandma Vi said, "It's not fair, Cen, but every West family member is a target. The Wests and the Rocklins go way back. We were allies once, but that's forever changed."

"Changed by what?"

Mom groaned. "Ignore her, Cen. She doesn't know what she's talking about."

We reached the outskirts of town and the scenery turned rural. The lush farmland changed to arid vineyards and finally forest as the road wound its way out of the valley and into the surrounding foothills.

The hills were once an affluent area of estate acreages, before the economic downturn that reversed the fortunes of many. Business never recovered, and many of the large estates were simply abandoned, too expensive to upkeep. Fortunes ebbed and flowed, but mostly they left town, never to return.

Grandma Vi, who had been sulking in the backseat all this time, finally broke the silence. "You should have told Cen, Ruby. You've put her—and all of us—in danger."

"Danger? Mom, is that true?"

Mom ignored me and turned the radio so loud that the whole car vibrated from the booming bass. It was a hard rock song with heavy bass and a screaming male lead singer. I covered my ears, but his voice grated and reverberated throughout every bone in my body. Since when did Mom listen to heavy metal?

Suddenly the radio went silent.

I lowered my hands from my ears, thankful that the music had stopped. My relief lasted only a split second. Then sparks flew from the dashboard as the radio smoked, and then caught on fire.

What if it spread? Would the gas tank explode?

"The curse!" I exclaimed. "Oh, my goodness, it's happening already."

"Oh, don't be ridiculous, Cen." Mom took one hand off the steering wheel and batted at the flames with her palm. "Now, help me put the fire out."

I pushed her hand away as the car careened over the center line. "Watch the road."

I looked around for something to smother the flames but the only thing handy was my purse. I slapped it against the dashboard in a futile attempt to extinguish the fire, but the flames grew larger and my melting purse stuck to my fingertips.

I snatched my hand away, but it was too late. My fingers stung from the flames and my purse had liquified into a sticky mess. The fire was real, but my so-called genuine leather purse was not.

As the flames crackled and sparked, Grandma Vi muttered a spell under her breath and extinguished the fire with a wave of her ghostly arm. "Gosh, that was hard! Cut the crap, Ruby. No more distractions and drama."

"Look who's talking. A ghost who can't mind her own business." Mom bit her lip and fought back tears.

"Stop fighting." I glanced down at my lap, where a big singe mark on my purse still smoldered. It was, quite literally, toast. I should have cast a spell instead of using my purse, but Mom's uncharacteristic behavior frightened me. So did Grandma Vi, setting this fire.

"You lit the car on fire! Talk about drama." Mom coughed as she waved away smoke.

Grandma Vi cleared her throat. "Casting spells used to be so easy. Boy, am I out of shape."

"You told me before that ghosts couldn't do magic—" Grandma Vi had always blamed Aunt Pearl for the periodic hauntings at our inn, claiming she had lost her witch powers. Truth seemed to be in short supply in my family.

"I save my spells for dire emergencies, like the situation we're in now. It was the only way I could get your attention." Grandma Vi floated toward the seat back and hovered between Mom and me. "If Ruby won't tell you about the curse, then I will. Listen carefully, because your life depends on it."

"Okay." Mom and Grandma Vi never fought, ever. Mom had somehow activated an ancient curse I knew nothing about, and Grandma Vi had set the car on fire. I was confused because everything was the opposite of normal, and Aunt Pearl wasn't even involved.

"Once upon a time there were two fam—"

"This isn't a fairy tale," Mom snapped.

"Fine, Ruby! Have it your way!" Grandma Vi said. "Long ago, when I was just a small child, the Rocklins and the Wests were each bestowed with supernatural powers. Equal powers. Together, the two families protected the vortex from unsavory characters and hid it from the uninitiated."

"The vortex is the reason we're witches?" I always wondered why we possessed supernatural powers when others didn't. Growing up, my questions always went unanswered. At some point, I simply stopped asking.

Grandma Vi nodded. "We agreed to be guardians of the vortex. In return we were given spellcasting powers."

Though I knew little about the source of our witchy talents, I knew much more about the vortex. I had even been in it once. The Westwick Corners vortex was a smaller version of other earthly vortexes, like Sedona, Arizona, and the most famous vortex of all, Stonehenge. Our vortex was lesser known, but like each of the earth's seven energy vortexes, it was a source of supernatural power for anyone nearby. It granted special powers, even travel through portals to other times and places.

Every self-respecting witch knew about the Westwick Corners vortex. It re-energized a witch's waning powers, kind of like a supernatural fountain of youth. It was like spellcasting on steroids. But vortexes also had a downside if you weren't careful. Their powers could be harnessed for either good or evil, and a vortex in the wrong hands could cause incalculable damage. As guardians, our job was to protect the vortex. In return, we were bestowed supernatural powers.

People generally dismissed vortexes as historical sites of pagan rituals or new age metaphysical nonsense. Our vortex was relatively unknown and had few visitors, so we had become complacent over time. Several years ago, desperate for tourists, we had attracted the attention of a malevolent witch. Tonya Plante had almost seized control of the vortex. Thankfully we quashed her plans to turn it into a luxury resort. Our negligence and desperation hadn't activated a curse then. Why was now so different?

"I was committed from birth to guard the vortex. I had no choice in the matter. Now I'm afflicted with a curse I know nothing about?" I leaned back in my seat and crossed my arms. My future had been decided without my input, which was totally unacceptable. Was there any part of my destiny that was not predetermined?

"It's not a big deal, Cen," Mom said brightly. "Together we guard this little vortex that no one ever visits. In return we get supernatural powers that we can do whatever we want with. It's a pretty good arrangement."

"Well, I quit," I said. "Being a witch is more of a burden than a benefit."

"You're not allowed to quit. It's hereditary," Mom said, fake cheeriness in her voice. "Nobody in their right mind quits being a witch. Plenty of women would switch places with you in an instant."

"Well, they can have the job. No one can force me to do a job I never asked for."

"Yes, they can, Cen. We made a collective West family vow, for evermore." Mom hit the gas again.

"Where are these Rocklin people? How did they get to quit and we don't?"

Mom said, "The Rocklins were, uh…downsized."

"I want to be downsized too."

Mom gasped. "Believe me, Cen, you do not want to be downsized. Erasing supernatural powers is very unpleasant and it can't be undone. The vortex is your calling, a lifetime commitment. Embrace it."

The only lifetime commitment I wanted was with Tyler, away from my crazy family.

Grandma Vi floated over Mom's right shoulder. "Tell her the truth, Ruby. Tell her about the war and why we seized control."

"Wait—what? The Wests battled the Rocklins?" All this time I believed that we were the only caretaker witches to guard the vortex. "You still haven't told me where the Rocklins went. What are you hiding?"

"They were banished to a top-secret location. I have no idea where," Grandma Vi interjected. "What I do know is that they are coming for us now. Your mother's actions have put us in danger."

"We all have to make a living," Mom snapped. "I don't see you generating any cash."

Grandma Vi's voice broke. "Give me a break—I'm dead! I worked my whole life to feed and clothe you, and all I get is ungrateful—"

I interrupted. "Stop fighting. Mom, why did you keep such a basic, relevant fact from me all my life?" Mom, Aunt Pearl, and even Grandma Vi—I was angry with all of them. They had deceived me for all these years.

Mom glanced over at me, looking sheepish. "I was just trying to protect you, Cen. Sorry. I never told you because that curse is ancient history. You know, I was just a child when the Rocklin battle took place. Your grandma was directly involved, so she's the one—"

"Stop blaming me for everything, Ruby."

Mom sighed. "Grandma can tell you the story. Just remember—she exaggerates."

Grandma Vi sighed. "If Ruby hadn't broken all the rules, there would be nothing to tell. But it is your right to know about the curse, since it impacts your life in a big way."

"Impacts me how? Are we in danger from the Rocklins?" I swallowed the lump in my throat as it dawned on me that Mom hadn't always kept me out of harm's way.

"Just saying the Rocklin name could call them back and endanger us, Cen. Just call them the black witches from now on, okay?"

"Okay. Does that make us the white witches?" I asked.

Grandma Vi nodded. "Sort of, though Pearl is in a bit of a grey zone. Witches get greedy just like regular folks. When the black witches tried to take over the vortex with black magic, we had to act. That's why two witch families were assigned to jointly protect the vortex: the Wests and those black witches. We were supposed to keep each other honest. It had worked for a time, but then our truce fell apart and things got pretty gruesome."

Mom stared straight ahead at the road, stone-faced and silent.

Grandma Vi nodded. "We, the white witches, triumphed

in the end. We barely won with the help of many white witches. The entire witch world was destabilized until we eventually settled on a pact. The Rock—I mean, the black witches—retained their supernatural powers but only if they left Westwick Corners and the vortex immediately. They kept their promise and left that same night. That was more than fifty years ago."

"The black witches got to leave and keep their witch powers, but we can't? That doesn't seem fair." I wondered what our promise was.

Silence.

"Such a long time ago," Mom said with a fake note of cheeriness. "To this day, they have never returned."

"That's because we didn't antagonize them by renting out their house, Ruby."

Mom shrugged. "They were banished. What good is the house to them? They should have just sold the place."

Grandma Vi glowed a transparent red with anger. "That house belongs to them forever, not you. Part of the pact allowed them to place a curse on our family, should we ever set foot on their property or try to seize absolute power. That's why their house still stands abandoned, yet available for their possible return. If we break the pact, they will return. Then we will be the banished ones."

The love of my life, my business, and my very soul were firmly entrenched in Westwick Corners. The thought of leaving Tyler, the newspaper, and the only home I had ever known terrified me. I pushed the thought from my mind. I had to stop whatever it was Mom had gotten us into.

Mom shifted her gaze from the road to me. "The

Rocklin mansion has so much potential. It's a fixer-upper of course, but nothing a little elbow grease can't—"

"Ruby! Eyes on the road!" Grandma Vi shrieked as we drifted over the center line and into the path of a semi-trailer barreling down on us from the other direction.

The truck honked and swerved to avoid us.

I gripped the door handle and braced for impact.

Mom swore under her breath as she steered back into her lane and lightened up on the gas pedal.

Collision averted, I turned around to check on Grandma Vi in the backseat.

Grandma Vi's aura had darkened to a deep purple. She gasped in short, quick sentences, clearly upset. "Our family is headed for disaster. And unless and until you have kids, well…the West family depends on you, Cen. We can't have the West family line die out."

Why wasn't my brother, Alan, ever subjected to these obligations? He always seemed to escape them. He lived a carefree life in London, England. True, he wasn't in a relationship, and had no interest in having kids. As a male, he didn't have the witchy powers the female West members had. Still, he always got a pass on pretty much everything.

Ugh. I had to stop feeling sorry for myself.

Sometimes being a witch was a curse in itself. Witchcraft benefits were well-known but infrequent. Nobody talked about the day-to-day restrictions we had to follow. "Are there other ways that we could be uh…gone? Could they kill us?"

"Not directly," Grandma Vi said. "But reactivating the curse has the same result of deadly misfortune for each of us. For the last time, Ruby, turn this car around. One step into that Rocklin place and we'll be signing our own death sentence."

"I will not," Mom said. "A lot of good came out of the fight. It's the reason WICCA was formed. Before that, it was like the Wild West, with no witch governing body, and no constitution and laws governing us."

"Breaking our promise unleashes the curse, Ruby. The black witches can and will return with a vengeance. They'll destroy us all, including you, Cen."

"But I wasn't even born when it happened."

Grandma Vi dismissed me with a wave of her hand. "We're all impacted by choices made by the generations before us, Cen. It's unfair, but they will turn us against each other, one by one. It will happen so gradually that we won't even know it's happening. Until it's too late."

A sense of dread enveloped me. "Like right now, with you and Mom fighting? Maybe it's happening already." Everything Mom was doing was so out of character.

"Yes, Cen. Try and talk some sense into your mom. It's not too late for us to do a reversal spell, but we'll need all of us to do it. Even your Aunt Pearl." Grandma Vi floated to the backseat, clearly distraught.

"Mom, maybe Grandma's right. Let's do that reversal spell." I turned around to look at Grandma Vi in the backseat, but her aura had already faded into nothingness. All this conflict was too much to bear.

Silence.

There wasn't a chance in hell of that happening. We were going to the Rocklin mansion, and there was no turning back.

* * *

MOM STOPPED the car in front of a pair of large black wrought iron gates that blocked the driveway entrance to the Rocklin Mansion. In the middle of each gate's scrollwork was an ornate, scripted initial 'R'. For the family with the unmentionable name, I assumed.

She turned to me. "Well, what do you think?"

Curse or no curse, the place gave me the creeps. I didn't want to argue, so instead I said, "It looks very elegant."

Though I had passed by the mansion many times, I had never glimpsed beyond the ten-foot iron fence, barely visible under the blackberry brambles and English ivy that smothered it like a death grip. Now the weeds were gone, and the fence had a fresh coat of black paint. Two security cameras were perched atop the fence, recording anyone passing through or near the gates.

On either side of the gates stood a pair of six-foot pyramid cedars and a group of potted winter pansies in full bloom. It was obviously Mom's witchcraft at work, though it seemed she hadn't had either the time or inclination to melt the frost off the new-looking asphalt. It was February though, and the icy driveway at least gave the place an air of authenticity.

Whatever secrets lay behind the locked gates would have to wait a little longer, since Mom had apparently forgotten her key. She swore under her breath as she lowered the driver's side window and softly whispered a spell.

As we drove through the gates and up the driveway, my chest tightened. Part of me wanted to jump from the car and retreat. But I also wanted to see the mysterious Rocklin mansion close up. If our family curse was real, then presumably it had already been activated during Mom's first visit to the Rocklin mansion. It was too late to back out. I still held a faint hope that Grandma Vi had invented her story to stop Mom's latest business venture. Except why would she? The curse couldn't affect Grandma Vi directly because she was already a ghost.

Or could it?

How odd that Grandma Vi had traveled with us in the car in the first place. I knew of only one other occasion when she had left the house since becoming a ghost, and that was because our lives were in jeopardy. Which they were again, if her claim was true. I shivered at the thought. I had so many questions, but voicing them would only provoke an argument, so I remained silent as we wound our way up the long driveway.

We rounded a curve, and I glimpsed the top of a steeply pitched roof. Judging by the height, the mansion was at least three storeys high.

I imagined room after room suddenly abandoned by its former occupants, never to return. Years of neglect added cobwebs and dust, once new furniture dusty and faded. Mom's spells would transform the place into something rentable, of course. If the curse was no big deal, then why had Mom been so secretive? Aunt Pearl and Grandma Vi were both afraid. That worried me since they rarely agreed on anything.

The driveway curved yet again and suddenly the mansion came into full view. The large three-storey house was imposing and palatial with its classic architecture. The sandblasted brick façade was accented with large white columns along a veranda that ran the entire width of the house. Large casement windows stood on either side of a set of large double entrance doors. The entrance was flanked with a pair of potted spiral-pruned evergreens that added to the formal symmetry.

Even the gardens looked spectacular despite the winter weather. Shrubs that bordered the circular driveway had been pruned into topiary bears, eagles, and other creatures. The landscaping added a touch of whimsy to counter the formal architecture, and it was all covered with a light dusting of snow. The place had the vibe of a glamorous yet trendy estate, with a little mystique thrown in. The old mansion had been fully restored to new condition and wouldn't have been out of place in the pages of *Homes & Gardens* magazine.

No doubt the renovations and updating had come from Mom's magic and not speedy contractors. Unlike Aunt Pearl's frivolous and sometimes vindictive use of witchcraft, Mom's spells always had a practical—and often beautiful—result. I remembered some very lean years growing up, and our survival always hinged on Mom's practical magic.

"Isn't it gorgeous, Cen? It's ours." Mom let out a contented sigh as she parked in the circular driveway behind a white Mercedes SUV.

"What do you mean, ours? You told me you leased it for a week."

"No, you misunderstood. I said we had guests for a week. I bought the place for a song. Just promise me you won't tell Pearl, because she's mad enough at me already."

"You bought it from the Rocklins?" A willing buyer and seller surely meant there was no curse.

"Uh…it's completely legal. I have title to the property."

"But Mom—what about the Rocklin curse? You bought it without consulting with any of us."

"One hundred percent my money, Cen. I don't see why I have to ask anyone's permission."

"The curse is why, Mom. That affects all of us."

Mom laughed nervously. "You don't believe all that nonsense, do you?"

"Curse or no curse, how will we manage everything? This is even bigger than the inn and it's miles away on the other side of town." There was no way I could add to my duties. My days were already full.

Mom turned to me. "We'll talk about it later. Right now, you're going to meet our very special guests, who checked in late last night. You're going to be thrilled! They're famous people with a great need for privacy, so promise me you'll keep their stay a secret."

"Who are they?" Why would anyone—let alone wealthy celebrities—choose Westwick Corners for a vacation in the dead of winter? Maybe I'd at least get a story out of it.

"You'll see soon enough. Follow me." She opened the door and stepped out of the car.

I carried the muffin basket and followed behind Mom across the driveway to the front door. As we reached the front steps, the front door swung open.

I couldn't believe who I saw.

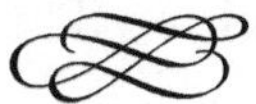

CHAPTER 4

*M*om grabbed my arm and whispered excitedly, "Our guests are Steve and Serena McCoy, the hottest couple in Hollywood!"

I froze in my tracks and gasped. *The Real McCoys* reality television show was number one in the ratings. Though I didn't watch the show myself, I instantly recognized the couple. Their faces were everywhere: in commercials, tabloid newspapers, and all over social media. It was pretty much impossible *not* to see them.

Once I regained my composure, I asked, "Why did they choose Westwick Corners in the dead of winter? We aren't exactly the Riviera, and the Rocklin mansion isn't the Waldorf Astoria, either."

"They wanted something different, Cen. Solitude and privacy."

That made sense—sort of. Steve McCoy had made millions as an ambulance-chasing lawyer who won multi-million-dollar malpractice lawsuits. Serena earned even more with her cosmetics, fragrance, and fashion brands. That success had morphed exponentially with their hit reality show.

They frequently clashed as they lived life to the fullest. The McCoys were real-life train wreck characters that people couldn't get enough of. Their relationship was more war than peace, and every aspect of their lives had been monetized. I suspected that their real purpose was filming a Valentine's Day-themed show.

Few days in the year caused such a romantic rollercoaster as Valentine's Day. A reality-show couple with a stormy relationship was the perfect prescription for people wanting to escape their own troubles. I imagined how it would play out. Serena would expect an elaborate gift, and Steve would fail to deliver.

Mom pulled hard on my arm. "Cen! Snap out of it."

"Ouch!" As I twisted to escape her grasp, my shoulder cracked. The pain jolted me back to reality.

"Everything okay?" Leaning against the intricately carved oak door was a breathtakingly beautiful woman with white-blonde hair, pulled back into a ponytail. Serena McCoy wore a hip-length angora sweater over faded jeans and fluffy white slippers. Despite her casual dress, she had an aura about her, a powerful presence of something I couldn't quite quantify. For the very first time, I experienced 'star-power' first-hand. It was every bit as magical as witchcraft.

I regained my composure and nodded, still speechless.

"Ruby, I am so glad we found you. We just love the place!" Serena McCoy clasped her palms together and smiled. She stepped back and placed one hand on the carved door, tracing her fingers over the intricate pattern of interwoven roses and leaves. "This is such a special place."

Mom beamed. "You're our very first guests. Oh, this is my daughter, Cendrine. I hope you don't mind me bringing her along. She works in the family business."

I opened my mouth but was still too star-struck to speak. Hollywood was famous for its beautiful people, but that beauty came from a bevy of stylists, makeup artists, and wardrobe consultants, working their magic behind the scenes. Airbrushed photographs, optimum lighting, and creative cinematography disguised the fact that in real life, movie stars were often plainer, shorter, and heavier.

Serena was a notable exception. She was even more beautiful and stunning in real life, despite any obvious trace of make-up. Her intense, emerald green eyes contrasted against her tanned, glowing complexion.

"There's nothing better than working with family, and nothing worse, either." Serena laughed, exposing a brilliant white smile. She stepped aside and motioned for us to enter. "Ladies, please come in out of the cold."

We stepped inside to a spacious foyer with a marble floor. A wide oak staircase stood to the left of the foyer, carved with the same intertwined rose and leaf pattern that graced the front door. Whether it was Art Deco or Art Nouveau, I wasn't sure, but I immediately recognized Mom's style. The staircase led up to a long, open hallway that overlooked the entryway.

The opposite side of the foyer opened into a large living room with a massive stone fireplace. The mantel was also carved with the same rose and leaf motif. Liberal sprinkles of witchcraft had restored the abandoned mansion to better than new, from the gleaming marble floors to the sparkling crystal chandeliers. There wasn't a cobweb or dust bunny in sight. Odd for a house that had sat vacant for decades.

"It's nice to finally relax after eight long months of filming." Serena smiled as she closed the door behind us. "Not that I'm complaining. Seven years ago, I was waiting tables at Nate's House of Pancakes." Serena's rise to fame was a rags-to-riches story. Her refusal of a ten-thousand-dollar tip from a customer had gone viral, and the rest was history. Her breakfast-serving at a highway truck-stop restaurant ended that day, replaced with modeling contracts, cosmetic deals, and walk-on sitcom roles. Soon after, she met Steve and the rest was the stuff of reality show legend.

"You're such an inspiration," Mom gushed. "I just love your show."

Serena waved her arm at our surroundings. "And I love all or your special touches, Ruby. Who is your interior decorator?"

Mom beamed. "I did it all myself. You'll find this is the perfect house. It's quiet and secluded so you can have all the privacy you need. It has every feature you asked for, even the outdoor pool."

Serena noticed my frown and said, "You must think we're crazy to want an outdoor pool in February, but Steve insisted on it. He has to swim his laps, and he says doing it outdoors in winter is invigorating."

That's not what I would call it, but then again, I found heated indoor pools too cold. An outdoor pool in February would give me a heart attack.

Mom pushed me forward. "Did I mention that Cen is a

local journalist? She just happens to be writing a piece about your show and I thought—"

Serena turned to me and flashed her perfect white teeth. "As a matter of fact, I just might have a story to break. Maybe you'll be the first to know."

I opened my mouth to reply but stopped myself. Instead, I handed the basket to Serena. Mom and I needed to talk, but not in front of guests.

Serena took the basket and sniffed. "Do I smell banana muffins?"

Mom beamed and nodded. "Fresh from the oven!"

Serena lifted the cloth that covered the basket and chose a muffin. She took a bite. "Mmmm…delicious!"

"I'll bring you more tomorrow," Mom said. "As long as it isn't too much of an intrusion."

"I would love that," Serena said. "Showbiz is exciting and all, but we really need some downtime. That's why we booked a weeklong stay. I may as well tell you my secret now." Serena glanced behind her to make sure no one was within earshot. She leaned in closer and whispered conspiratorially. "Steve and I really want this Valentine's Day to be extra special. We've decided to renew our vows here."

Mom's hand flew to her chest. "Ooh…that's so romantic! You'll need flowers, champagne, and a cake. I'll take care of everything. Do you need it catered?"

Serena shook her head. "Catering won't be necessary. It's just a small, casual ceremony. Flowers would be nice though."

"Consider it done," Mom said.

The Rocklin Mansion seemed more suited to a gala wedding than a private vow renewal ceremony. Even

Mom's magical touches couldn't make the cavernous mansion cozy, let alone intimate. On the other hand, the house was much smaller than Serena's TV reality show house, so it probably felt cozy by comparison. I had to admit, it was pretty.

The vow renewal ceremony was almost certainly a reality show episode. How could it not be? This couple lived their relationship entirely on screen, with frequent fights and constant conflict. I just hoped Mom had gotten a damage deposit because absolutely nothing was off-limits on *The Real McCoys*. Whether it was just an episode or real life, it was a story-worthy scoop.

"Oh…there is one more thing." Serena turned to me. "I need a photographer. I have a proposal. I'll grant your newspaper exclusive rights to the story in return for a few photographs. Your photographer can do double duty."

"I don't have a photog—"

Mom cut me off. "Cen's photographer is very talented. He's won several regional awards for his work."

"Fantastic." Serena waved her hand. "As for the flowers, a few vases for the living room would be nice, along with a bouquet for me."

Mom made an imaginary checkmark with her index finger. "I'll come back shortly with some flower ideas to choose from."

Serena's eyes widened. "You're so efficient! I'm so glad I found you and this lovely place."

Footsteps echoed in the hall, adding to my growing sense of panic.

"Hon, have you seen my reading glasses?" Steve McCoy emerged from the hallway.

Despite the cold February weather, he wore a short-sleeved t-shirt, board shorts, and flip-flops. He was noticeably older than Serena, a stocky yet fit man with closely-cropped grey hair. He stopped suddenly when he saw us. "Sorry, I didn't know we had guests."

"These are the owners of the place, Steve. Ruby West and her daughter, Cendrine. I think your eyeglasses are on the kitchen counter."

After we shook hands, Steve placed his arm around Serena's waist and pulled her closer. Their affection for each other seemed genuine, a stark contrast to their warring, on-screen hostility. But contentment didn't win ratings, and reality TV shows thrived on conflict and exaggeration.

Serena held out her muffin. "Taste this muffin from Ruby, Steve."

Steve broke off a piece of muffin and turned to Mom. "These smell great. Serena told you about our plans to renew our vows?"

Mom smiled. "We'll make it a day to remember. Oh... Serena, if you need a dress there's a nice little shop in town —Bunny's Key to Fashion."

Where I bought my Valentine's Day dress. The dress I couldn't zip up.

The last episode in the reality show's season had ended in a cliff-hanger, with Steve and Serena headed for divorce court, the exact opposite of the loving couple standing before us now. The vows were surely another contrived plot twist. Faking a breakup was just as good for ratings as a reconciliation. It made a juicy feature story too.

Serena leaned into Steve. "I'm liking this place. Maybe we can extend our stay."

Steve finished his muffin morsel and selected another muffin from the basket. He took a small bite and savored it. "Delicious. Can I get the recipe, or is it a family secret?"

"You bake?" I had finally found my voice again.

"Once in a while, whenever I find time. We don't get much downtime when we're filming. Which is probably good, or I'd be carrying an extra fifty pounds like I was before the show. Right, hon?"

Serena laughed. "Along with Steve's crash diet, he has this strict exercise regime. Fifty laps every day, in a freezing outdoor pool."

Steve flushed. "I'm 2 hours late today. I'm usually in the pool by 8 a.m. This place is so relaxing that I'm finding it hard to motivate myself."

Mom beamed. "We won't keep you. I'll be back in a jiffy with some floral options. If you need anything else in the meantime, just call."

We had just turned to leave when a loud male voice boomed from upstairs. "Shut the damn door. It's freezing in here."

Jason, Steve's son from his first marriage, glared down at us from the second-floor landing. Jason's recent cut from the reality show was explained as drug dealing and addiction in a special intervention episode. Whether Jason's role as a drug-addicted dealer on *The Real McCoys* was real or contrived, I didn't know. He was just as entitled and rude in real life though.

Steve's face darkened as he spoke in a hushed voice.

"Ignore Jason's rudeness. He got kicked out of rehab—again. He has nowhere to go and he's miserable."

"The vows are a surprise," Serena whispered. "We aren't telling Jason beforehand. We're afraid he'll sabotage things."

"We won't say a word." I felt embarrassed to be included in the family drama.

Jason stomped down the stairs, stopping a few steps from the bottom. "Who are these people? You said we couldn't have visitors."

Mom and I exchanged uneasy glances. It was weird to be talked about like we weren't even there.

Serena answered for us. "These are our hosts, Ruby West and her daughter Cendrine. They own this place."

Jason gave Mom a cursory glance, then turned his attention to me. His eyes traveled slowly up my body, pausing a little too long just below my neckline. "Could use some fixing up."

Did he mean me, or the Rocklin mansion? Either way, it was incredibly insulting. I fought the urge to respond with a comment I would regret later.

"Any bars in this town?" Jason's eyes remained on me as he grabbed a muffin from the basket in Serena's hand. He swallowed the muffin in two bites and dropped the wrapper in the basket before wiping his hands on his jeans.

"The only place open is The Witching Post, just across town." I didn't want any more condescending comments, so I omitted the fact that we owned the bar. The rustic bar would surely disappoint Jason's high standards, but maybe that was a good thing. One visit and he wouldn't be back.

"Witching Post? That's the stupidest name I ever heard."

Jason pushed his way in between Mom and I, hitting my shoulder and throwing me off balance.

"Ouch!" I stumbled a few feet before my shoulder hit the wall. I quickly regained my balance, but my shoulder ached from the impact.

Jason either didn't notice or didn't care. He swung the front door open with such force that it hit the wall with a thud.

He didn't bother closing it behind him.

We all stood in silence, watching Jason run down the front steps and across the driveway toward a new-looking red Porsche with a dented front fender. He paused by the driver's door and stared defiantly back at us.

As if he dared somebody to stop him.

"Here we go again." Steve sighed.

Jason opened the driver's door and hopped in. He turned the ignition and started the engine. Loud music blared from the car's stereo system through the open driver's side door.

Steve walked to the open front door and shouted over the bass heavy music. "Where are you going, Jason?"

"Gotta take care of some business." Jason revved the engine.

Steve yelled after Jason. "You've come this far, Jason. Don't screw it up."

Jason revved the Porsche's engine again before putting the car in reverse and backing up. He drove the car around the circular driveway and stopped in front. He rolled down his window and shouted over the idling engine. "It's my life. I'll do whatever the hell I want." He turned the stereo even louder. Heavy metal music boomed from the car speakers.

The Porsche's tires squealed as he stepped on the gas and sped away down the driveway.

It was clear from Jason's outburst that the McCoys' TV drama wasn't entirely fake. They couldn't escape their real-life family drama, even on vacation. They probably chose our out-of-the-way town so nobody saw their dysfunctional family up close.

Mom broke the awkward silence. "Don't worry, we won't say a word. We would never compromise your privacy."

Steve let out a nervous laugh. "We surrendered our privacy when we started the show. Our family is an open book. But still…stuff like this is kind of embarrassing sometimes."

Serena nodded. "Sometimes I wonder if the show is the cause of Jason's troubles. This was his fifth stint in rehab. Growing up famous is hard. The drugs are a coping mechanism. We do everything we can to help, but he's got to help himself first."

"Jason's had everything handed to him," Steve said. "Yet he's so self-destructive."

I felt a pang of guilt. "Sorry I mentioned the bar. At least there are no drugs in town."

Serena sighed. "Drugs are everywhere, even in this little town. Jason will find them, that's for sure. That's the one thing I've learned in the last seven years. At least we didn't end up buying him the more expensive Porsche that he wanted. He crashed this one within a week and expects us to pay to fix it. He's got an out-of-control drug problem and doesn't show up for filming half the time, so we were forced to write him out of the show."

Mom gasped. "All those stints in rehab didn't work?"

Serena shook her head. "They work for awhile, but he always relapses. Now he simply refuses to go anymore. We can't help him unless he wants to get better. We don't know what to do."

If Serena and Steve really wanted to help Jason recover from his addiction, broadcasting his struggles on network TV seemed the wrong way to go about it. Airing family struggles was good for ratings, but it betrayed so much trust in the process. I felt a tiny bit sorry for Jason.

Serena was Jason's stepmother, but she was barely ten years older than him. Rumor had it that Jason resented Steve marrying Serena less than a year after his mother's accidental death eight years ago.

Mom cleared her throat and said in an artificially cheery voice, "Lots to do, so we'd better get going, Cen."

Once we were back in the car I asked, "Why do people renew their vows, Mom? What's the point?"

Mom turned the key in the ignition and started the car. "They are reaffirming their commitment to each other. Sometimes it's done after a bad patch, or maybe to celebrate a milestone, like a 10-year anniversary. Maybe they never had a real ceremony in the first place. Remember episode 3? Steve and Serena were too busy filming the show to have a real wedding, so they just had that small ceremony on the city hall steps."

I laughed. "You know way too much about these people. You're obsessed with them."

Mom shrugged and put the car in gear. "I believe in happy endings, Cen. I don't believe there is a Rocklin curse.

Ignore whatever Pearl and Grandma say, because we've got a very bright future ahead of us."

"More like no future," Grandma Vi snapped from the backseat.

"Speaking of the future, where do I find a photographer?" I asked.

"Aunt Pearl just got a new camera," Mom said. "She'd be absolutely perfect!"

She'd be a perfect train wreck. Which, in a way, *was* a picture-perfect Real McCoy's event.

CHAPTER 5

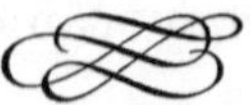

I traced my finger over the car stereo's melted volume knob and wondered whether the McCoys had brought us good fortune or bad. Mom stared straight ahead, both hands gripping the steering wheel as we drove back through town. Grandma Vi sulked in the backseat. Her spell had extinguished the fire, but the radio no longer worked. The silence was uncomfortable. I considered doing a radio repair spell as a favor to Mom, but that would only trigger another argument.

Instead, I focused my thoughts on the Real McCoys feature article. Any story about vow renewals should start with the blossoming of Steve and Serena's fairy-tale romance. How my story unfolded depended upon two possible scenarios: either the vow renewal ceremony was real, or else it was just a made-up story for *The Real McCoys* reality TV show. I wouldn't know which until the actual ceremony, but either way it didn't matter much. Most of the article would be background material from the reality show, and I'd just fill in the blanks later.

If the vow renewal was genuine, I'd write a good-news story that contrasted with their on-screen hostility toward each other. If the vows were a staged reality show ceremony, then the story would write itself. There would be insults and destruction, and I would simply record the action.

The story had pretty much landed in my lap. I couldn't wait to start writing it, but first I had to finish the final edits on my Valentine's Day feature. The Rocklin curse seemed more fiction than reality. Today had turned out to be a lucky day.

* * *

WHEN MOM finally turned into our driveway and drove up the long, winding road to the inn at the top of the hill, my heart sank. Jason's red Porsche was parked adjacent to a large white van and a truck near the separate building that housed The Witching Post Bar and Grill. It was unusual at this time of year to see vehicles in the parking lot at midmorning. Maybe some contractors had stopped in for an early lunch.

At least Lucky was bartending today instead of Aunt Pearl. The less Aunt Pearl interacted with anyone, the better, particularly somebody as bad-tempered as Jason McCoy.

I hurried behind Mom as she strode across the parking lot toward the front steps of the inn. "Aunt Pearl can't be the photographer. You know she won't set foot on the Rocklin property."

Mom turned and threw her arms up and snapped at me. "That's right, I forgot. Well, then who, Cendrine? Do you have a solution? I can't do everything myself!"

"Uh…maybe Lucky could do it?" I cringed as I waited for Mom's response. She never, ever lost her temper, especially not with me. She was like a totally different person right now, and it scared me.

She turned at the foot of the stairs, her hands on her hips. "Lucky? You can't be serious!"

I shrugged. "Why not? It keeps Aunt Pearl busy bartending and away from interfering with the McCoys. That solves two problems. We'll just tell her that Lucky called in sick or something."

Mom's shoulders sagged. "Okay, fine. You coordinate it with Lucky. But he better not be a no-show."

"He won't, I promise. I'll even drive him to the Rocklin place myself."

Mom's shoulders slumped like she carried the weight of the world. Then she turned and trudged up the stairs without another word.

I called after her. "I know you're working hard, Mom. I promise I'll help more."

Mom turned. Her hand flew to her mouth. She looked as if she was about to cry. "I-I'm sorry I got mad, Cen. It's just that…sometimes I feel like I'm the only one holding all of us together. I run the inn, do all the cooking, and pay the bills only to get zero support. And then with Pearl and your grandma criticizing everything I do… I'm a little stressed out with everything right now."

"Don't worry, Mom, I'm here." Mom really should have consulted the rest of us before committing to her high stakes venture, but we were already in the midst of it and it was too late to turn back. The next twenty-four hours could make or break us. Everything else just had to wait.

Like the curse, which seemed more and more real by the minute.

Mom glanced down at her watch and sighed. "Maybe this is just too much for all of us. I hope I haven't made a terrible, terrible mistake."

CHAPTER 6

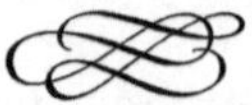

$\mathcal{M}$om and I sat in the inn's dining room. We were discussing the arrangements for Steve and Serena's vow renewal ceremony when Aunt Pearl stormed in.

"Over my dead body!" Aunt Pearl marched over to our table and wagged her finger at Mom. "The Rocklin curse will ruin us. I'm not risking my life over a few bucks."

Mom looked up from the glossy catalog of flower arrangements she had been showing us and frowned. "We need the money, Pearl. Our bookings have collapsed in the last few months. Are you even aware that we're facing financial ruin? We're lucky to get visitors at all. I don't see you generating any income."

"It's not worth endangering our lives, Ruby. Leave the Rocklin place alone, before it's too late." Aunt Pearl tapped her foot as she waited for an answer.

"Either we do or we starve to death. The McCoy's are

just a regular family," Mom said. "Except that they happen to be famous. They've brought along a few employees who will stay here at the inn. In a week they'll be gone. All the McCoys want is a nice quiet Valentine's Day. Oh, and they've asked me to help them renew their vows."

"They've got a film crew, Ruby! There's a van filled with equipment in the parking lot. Don't lie to me. This isn't a vow renewal, it's a publicity stunt."

Mom hadn't mentioned the crew. What other secrets had Mom kept from us?

Mom fake-smiled at Aunt Pearl. "Pearl, can you do the flowers? Maybe some white and red roses, and a pink and white balloon archway?"

Aunt Pearl stomped her foot. "I am *not* doing another one of your stupid balloon archways. You two have been planning this for months, haven't you?"

I waved my hands in protest. "I only found out about *The Real McCoys* on the drive over to the Rocklin place."

Aunt Pearl's eyes narrowed as she glared at us. "You really think some reality TV show is worth risking our very existence as witches? How much did they pay you?"

Mom's face reddened but she remained silent.

"What is it then? Did they offer you both roles on the show?"

"You've got it all wrong, Aunt Pearl." I disagreed with Mom's actions, but she always had our best interests at heart. "They didn't say anything about filming, and we aren't part of the cast. Steve and Serena just wanted a quiet little getaway."

Aunt Pearl rolled her eyes. "Oh, so now you're on a first-name basis? Nice try, Cen. You're both in cahoots. Your thirst for fame and riches is endangering our very existence as witches. I won't have any part of this. Get your own stupid balloons and flowers."

"I'm not—" I stopped mid-sentence, ashamed. Sure, Mom had been deceptive. But any fallout from the curse—if it was actually real—seemed vague. The curse was likely just fantastical legend blown all out of proportion. Mom had always protected me from harm. If the curse was truly something to fear, she would have told me years ago.

Curse or no curse, the real issue was trust. Why hadn't anyone in my family told me about the Rocklin curse before today? I couldn't ignore the fact that Grandma Vi and Aunt Pearl seemed genuinely terrified. That, in turn scared me. Aunt Pearl was the most fearless person I knew. If she was afraid, there had to be a good reason, and Mom should have informed me so I could draw my own conclusions.

I cleared my throat. "The McCoys will be gone in a few days, Aunt Pearl. You won't even see them." I omitted any mention of their son, who was at this very moment getting drunk at The Witching Post.

Aunt Pearl snorted. "How nice that our guests can relax as our lives are torn apart."

Mom threw her arms up in frustration. "The income from our guests allow us to live like this, Pearl." Mom waved her hand around our rustic dining room. The room was large but modestly furnished. The four large oak dining tables were worn but functional, repurposed from a bankrupt restaurant. The self-serve coffee and snack station beside the kitchen door was utilitarian, built by a local handyman. The dining room was more quaint than grand. But it served its purpose.

"We'll be lucky to live another day," Aunt Pearl muttered.

Mom shook her head. "Stop being so negative, both of you. They paid double our usual rate, in advance too."

"Ruby, there's not enough money in the world to compensate for triggering that curse."

"There is no curse, Pearl. Have you ever seen any evidence of it the whole time we've lived here?" Mom answered her own question. "No, you haven't."

Aunt Pearl's eyes narrowed. "The curse is dormant only because the Rocklins left town. Sure, that was decades ago, but one mistake and it gets reactivated. I'm the one who has kept that curse in check all these years, but does anyone appreciate that? No!" She shook her head.

"Oh, so now you're our saviour?" Mom said. "Really Pearl, you're ridiculous."

"Mom, stop."

Mom crossed her arms. "I'm not giving in this time. Pearl, stop and think about it. There is no external force that can take our powers away. Our powers aren't strictly hereditary. You know that too, Cen. Spells and witchcraft powers don't come to you, they come from you. We each spend thousands of hours honing our spell craft. We earned these powers, spell by spell, hour by hour and day after day of practice. Yes, we were given a gift, but our powers developed more from hard work than anything else."

Mom was right. While I was grateful for my supernatural abilities, I hadn't chosen the complication of being a witch. I had reluctantly accepted my responsibility at first, but eventually practised in secret just to meet Aunt Pearl's impossible standards. Every spell, potion, and herbal tincture had been hard earned. Success hadn't happened on its own.

One question still nagged at me. I turned to Mom. "The Rocklins really did leave town, didn't they?"

"Well…yes. People move for all kinds of reasons. Mom's tone was artificially upbeat.

Aunt Pearl said, "People don't move in the dead of night on a whim and leave their possessions behind, Ruby. You know why the Rocklins left, and Cen deserves the truth."

"She knows enough for now. The rest is a story for another day." Mom turned on her heels and walked briskly into the kitchen, slamming the door behind her.

Aunt Pearl turned to me, eyes dark with worry. "When you choose sides, choose wisely, Cendrine. Whatever happens next can't be undone."

CHAPTER 7

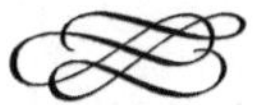

Ring-ring! Ring-ring! Ring-ring!

"Ouch!" Startled by the bell at the front desk under which I was kneeling, I jerked my head up and hit the counter. I extricated myself and stood up.

"It's about time I got some help." A bejewelled hand shoved a wad of papers across the inn's check-in desk. "I've got a reservation for twenty-four rooms, non-smoking."

I rubbed the sore spot on my head, where a lump was already forming. "Uh...that can't be right. The Westwick Corners Inn only has 8 rooms. We couldn't have possibly booked you twenty-four rooms."

I looked into the green eyes of a stunningly beautiful woman with long red hair. She leaned against the counter, closing the space between us.

Her eyes bored into mine as she tapped the papers with her index finger.

"Read this right here. We reserved twenty-four rooms. Not eight rooms. *Twenty-four rooms.*"

"Our rooms are quite spacious. If people want to share a—"

"Absolutely not," she said. "The crew always get private rooms, and that's what we reserved. You need to fix this immediately."

Mom hadn't mentioned any of this. Inside I fumed, but I forced a polite smile. "I think there's been a mix-up. The nearest hotel of that size is in Shady Creek, an hour away."

"Not acceptable," the woman snapped. She stepped back and looked for somebody else more helpful than me. She was casually but stylishly dressed in jeans, heels, and an emerald green sweater that matched her intense eyes.

She was going to rip me to shreds because no matter what I said or did, I simply didn't have twenty-four suites to offer. The day was a disaster already and it wasn't even noon yet. "I wish I could help but we only have—"

She waved her hands, palms out in protest. "Stop making excuses and give me the damn rooms."

My pulse pounded as I unfolded the paper. It was a reservation all right, but it was for a different hotel in a neighboring town. "I see what's happened. You reserved The Western Inn at Shady Creek. You're not the first person to mix us up. If you'd like, I can call them, Miss—"

"Abby Monroe. I'm Serena McCoy's personal assistant. Another town is not an option, and it's not what we arranged." Abby looked around to a tall, muscular man standing just inside the inn's front door. He gave an almost imperceptible nod as he shifted his stance.

The man looked oddly familiar, but I couldn't place

where I'd seen him. He had to be well over six-foot-five, because the top of his head reached the doorframe. He had the physique of a steroid-pumped bodybuilder, with arms so muscular that they hung not straight down by his side, but slightly out at an angle. I guessed he was part of the McCoys' security detail, though it was odd that he wasn't at the house with them. The presence of the cast and crew pretty much confirmed my suspicions that the McCoys' simple vow renewal wouldn't really be all that simple.

I drew in a deep breath. The customer was always right, especially a wrong one. I had to defuse the situation somehow. "Abby, you're in luck because all eight of our suites are vacant. I can give you those rooms right now. Unfortunately, there are no other places to stay in Westwick Corners. Can some of your crew stay in the next town?"

Abby shook her head and shoved a paper across the desk. She jabbed a finger at the letterhead. "You're wrong. This has to be the place. Even the GPS directed us here."

My face flushed as several other men and women entered the lobby. Arguing wouldn't solve the situation. Panic soared inside me as the small area was now crowded with people and loud voices. I took several deep breaths and reread the paper.

Sure enough, printed under the wrong hotel name and logo was our address. This made no sense, but I had to somehow fix things. One way or another, I needed to find twenty-four rooms, right now.

I looked up at Abby and fake-smiled. "That is odd. I don't know how that happened but don't worry, we'll get it all sorted out."

Mom, standing in the hallway, overheard us and walked

over. She joined me behind the counter. "Get what sorted out?"

I explained the situation and introduced Abby.

"Not a problem," Mom said brightly. "You're in luck because we've got another eight rooms in the annex. Some of you will have to double up, but they're very large suites. Will that work?"

Abby sighed. "It'll have to do, I guess. "We've got a busy day tomorrow."

MOM'S 'ANNEX' turned out to be Pearl's Charm School. Her witchcraft quickly transformed the building with a new façade and partitions to make another eight rooms, and somehow she won Abby over with her compromise. The rooms lacked the character of the inn, but the building looked tidy and new with a fresh coat of paint and some potted cedars out front. Best of all, it was a stone's throw across the parking lot from the inn and the Witching Post Bar and Grill, where they could unwind a bit.

Now all we had to do was explain the temporary expropriation of Pearl's Charm school to Aunt Pearl, who would have a fit. How had this hotel room mix-up occurred in the first place? Was this another of Mom's secrets? Or was it due to something more sinister, like the Rocklin curse?

CHAPTER 8

After a few frantic minutes, the entire McCoy entourage were checked into their rooms. It hadn't been easy. There were heated arguments over who had to share a room and who didn't, but Abby eventually sorted things out with several adjustments. Abby and the muscular security man, who turned out to be the McCoy's chauffeur, would stay at the Rocklin Mansion with the McCoys, as would Steve's stepson Jason. The original plan of Jason staying with the crew had surprised me. On the other hand, maybe Jason wanted to keep a little distance from his family.

Back in the kitchen, I sat at the breakfast nook, intent on finishing my Valentine's Day feature article. It just needed a few finishing touches, but I couldn't focus. I was preoccupied with a curse that Mom refused to acknowledge. Maybe I could find some information on the Rocklin family in old issues of the Westwick Corners Weekly or, failing that, the library's historical records. A family abandoning their mansion and leaving town in the middle of the night would have been newsworthy in a small town like ours. It was a starting point, at least.

My fingers were poised above the keyboard, about to type into the search bar when a gust of cold air swooshed over my head. Grandma Vi floated above me. Her semi-transparent form shimmered, swathed in a purple velvet cloak that swirled as she moved. She stared intently down at my laptop on the table beneath her.

"I'm proofreading for you, dear." Grandma Vi gripped an eraser-tipped pencil with both hands and jabbed clumsily at the screen. "You repeated a word in the second paragraph, Cen. I'm pressing as hard as I can, but for some reason, it won't erase."

She pressed the screen so hard that she lost her grip on the pencil. It dropped onto the keyboard with a thud. She waved her hand with a flourish at the screen. "It worked! I just had to press the right button!"

I gasped. The screen that had been filled with a wall of black type seconds earlier was now blank. I pressed the up arrow, then the down arrow as a sense of panic rose up inside me. "What the—did you just—?"

"Uh-oh. Where did all those words go? I only meant to delete one misspelled word, not the whole thing. Sorry, Cen." She recited a rewind spell, then stopped mid-sentence. "I can't think of the exact spell to get it back."

"It's okay. It's a simple fix." I pressed the 'undo' command on the keyboard.

Nothing happened. The blank screen glared at me, unchanged. "That should have worked. Did you save it?"

"Save what?" Grandma Vi squinted at the screen. "You know I don't like computers."

"Never mind, Grandma. I hadn't pressed the 'save' button yet, so I should have been able to undo what you did. I have no idea what happened."

Grandma Vi frowned. "Oh dear. The Rocklin curse is what happened. Fix it with a spot of witchcraft. Try a reversal spell."

My pulse raced as I muttered the reversal spell under my breath.

Nothing.

Beads of sweat formed on my forehead. My Valentine's Day issue—a week's worth of work—had been permanently deleted. I clicked on the computer's trash bin icon.

Empty.

Where on earth did my file go?

If only I hadn't procrastinated with just a few minutes of work left.

I swore under my breath and clicked the undo button again and again, knowing it was futile. I should have been able to undo the deletion, or even retrieve an older version of my file. Yet I couldn't. The file was completely gone from my computer. Witchcraft was definitely involved.

Not Grandma Vi's witchcraft, of course. She could barely cast spells as a ghost. She had just been trying to help. She would never knowingly sabotage my efforts. Mom wouldn't either.

Aunt Pearl was another story. She would love to shut down *The Westwick Corners Weekly* and force me to focus more on witchcraft. She always held out hope that her magical interference could bring me over to her side. But destroying my work in progress was too extreme even for her. And there were no other witches in town.

I massaged my forehead in the hopes of quashing the pounding headache I now had.

"Try the reversal spell again, Cen. You probably missed a word," Grandma Vi said.

"Worth a shot." I was doubtful but I had no other options. I took a deep breath and recited the reversal spell, slowly and carefully this time. I was halfway through the second line when the outside door flew open with such force that it banged against the wall.

"Something wrong?" Aunt Pearl entered the kitchen and kicked off her boots by the door. "Why are you just standing around instead of working?"

"My Valentine's Day file just disappeared for no reason." I watched carefully for her response.

Aunt Pearl shrugged. "The reason is the Rocklin curse. No great loss, since no one reads your articles anyway. It might as well be written by ghosts."

Grandma Vi glared at her. "Ghosts can write. Well, dictate at least. I just need someone to press the keys for me."

"It's not the curse and I can get it back,' I said. "Quiet, so I can concentrate."

Aunt Pearl mocked me in a sarcastic tone, "Quiet so she can concentrate! I'll have you know that a good witch operates in all kinds of conditions and doesn't let distractions—"

I plugged my ears and recited the reversal spell, this time in its entirety. Seconds later the screen filled with red hearts and valentines wishes.

I sighed with relief as I checked the text. It was my latest version, all intact. "Thank goodness it's back."

Grandma Vi clapped her transparent hands. "Well done, Cen! You're an amazing witch."

"She's passable," Aunt Pearl grumbled.

Grandma Vi ignored her. "Your Valentine's Day issue is such a great idea, Cen. I can't wait to read the rest." Grandma Vi hovered over my laptop once more, reading the valentine messages aloud. Once again, she gripped a pencil in her transparent hand.

Not wanting a repeat delete disaster, I conjured up a newsprint paper copy for Grandma Vi and also one for Aunt Pearl. I placed Grandma Vi's copy carefully in the center of the table and opened it up to the first page of the valentines. She'd have to stir up a windstorm to turn pages, but I was ready to help. I couldn't handle any more complications.

"I'm not reading this drivel." Aunt Pearl rolled her copy into a weapon and chucked it at my head. I caught it before it made contact and placed it on the table.

Grandma Vi looked up from her copy and giggled. "Ooh, look at this one: You are my Pearly Pearl, Love Earl. Gee, I wonder who that's for?"

We both turned to Aunt Pearl.

"Give me that!" Aunt Pearl's cheeks flushed a deep crimson. She snatched Grandma Vi's copy off the table and held the paper at arm's length, squinting to read the valentine messages.

"Oh, my Pearly Pearl. How adorable!" Grandma Vi floated a few feet off the floor, howling with laughter.

Aunt Pearl shoved the paper into my chest. "Geez, Cendrine. You're a lousy poet."

"I didn't write it; your boyfriend did. It's Earl's valentine wish for his sweetheart."

Aunt Pearl flushed. "Earl would never do something ridiculous like this. Your cheap thrills are just as bad as that stupid reality show."

"Why don't you ask Earl about it?" I smiled. "There is one mysterious valentine. It's an anonymous full-page ad to surprise a special someone. I can't figure out who it's from, or who it's meant for."

Mom came in from the dining room. "Who is what meant for?"

"It's a secret valentine, Mom. An anonymous well-wisher paid for a two-page spread." I pointed to the center spread in Grandma Vi's newspaper. The font was large enough for a ninety-year-old to read without reading glasses.

"Who's it from?" Mom asked.

I shrugged. "There was no name attached to the unmarked envelope that was slipped under my office door after hours yesterday." I didn't mention the five hundred dollars in cash that accompanied it. It was more than the ad cost, and I hoped to eventually return the excess funds.

"Ri-dic-u-lous!" Aunt Pearl marched over to the kitchen island and poured herself a cup of coffee from the carafe.

Mom came over to the table. "Well, what does the valentine say?"

I opened the paper and placed it in the centre of the table so we could all read it. "It's really sweet. You'll love it."

I read the short passage aloud:

. . .

*I LOVE YOU, **Honey***
  But I got no money,
  No means to survive,
  I live in a dump,
  I'm kind of plump,
  But will you be my valentine?

WITH NO ROOF over my head
  I might well be dead
  But you and me, you'll see
  We'll thrive
  In this dive,

WE'LL MAKE some hay
  Live happy days
  Have love divine
  If you'll be my valentine.

AUNT PEARL SCOFFED. "What kind of loser writes crap like that? It's horrible!"

"That's so sweet," Mom said. "Saying that I don't have much, but everything I have is yours. It's adorable."

"Argh!" Grandma Vi abruptly fell and crashed onto the table, her levitation gone. Her transparent form squirmed as she slowly rolled off the table and onto the bench seat.

"Grandma, are you okay?" I focused my thoughts and

tried to re-levitate her. I had done similar mental gymnastics before, mostly while practising my witchcraft. This time though, she didn't budge.

She nodded wearily. "It's the Rocklin curse, reactivated. I told you to leave that place alone, Ruby."

Mom's mouth dropped open in shock, but she didn't say anything.

Suddenly the room shifted and blurred. Walls cracked, dishes clattered to the floor, and the air grew thick with dust. I could barely see across the room. The haze cleared just as quickly, but it revealed that the breakfast nook we had gathered around had morphed into a picnic table.

A drop of water landed on my wrist. I looked upward and saw sky through a gaping hole in the ceiling. Highly unusual, since we were on the first floor of our three-storey inn. The giant hole in our ceiling aligned with a hole in the second-floor ceiling, and above that, the roof above the third floor. The sky was filled with storm clouds that had just started to spit rain.

Mom gasped. "Oh my, the guests! What if someone steps into the hole? One of our guests could die!"

As I stared upward in distress, the seam of my dress ripped.

Aunt Pearl pointed at my stomach. "Cen! You just gained thirty pounds!"

Grandma Vi spoke, her voice a whisper. "Oh my—that was a curse you recited, not a valentine poem, Cen. Everything you read aloud is happening to us right now. We literally have no roof over our head. This is all part of the Rocklin curse."

I shook my head. "It's just a coincidence."

"All our worst fears have come true!" Mom cried. "Instead of health, wealth, and happiness we've got sick, poor and sad. And fat."

My lower lip trembled as I fought the urge to cry.

Aunt Pearl frowned. "I warned you, Ruby. But you wouldn't listen."

Nobody said anything.

A few misspoken words had brought catastrophe. Now our fully booked inn was damaged, and our spell-casting abilities were threatened as well. The Rocklin curse was real, and it was already wreaking havoc. We were invincible together, but torn apart, we were powerless to fight it. Whatever came next could determine our future as witches for generations to come.

CHAPTER 9

I glanced upward at the ceiling's gaping hole. Mom had checked each room, but the only good news was that all our guests had gone out for lunch. They would return sooner or later, and everything had to be fixed before they returned.

Mom was furious. "You're behind this, Pearl. Whether you like paying guests or not, we need the money. Fix this roof before you drive our guests away."

Aunt Pearl walked over to the table, a solemn expression on her face. "You know it's not me, Ruby. It's the curse. You put us all in danger by renting out the Rocklin place."

I grabbed Mom's hand with my left hand and Aunt Pearl's hand with my right. "Enough of the blame game. Too late to do anything about that now. Let's combine forces and see if we can fix the roof." Grandma Vi closed the circle, and we recited the reversal spell, this time in unison.

It took all our efforts, and several tries, but we managed

to reverse the ceiling to its pre-spell condition. That done, I raced to the window to check on the annex. Thankfully it remained unaltered, still in its newly converted state.

"Whew! I'm exhausted." I collapsed into the breakfast nook. I craved a nap, and it wasn't even lunchtime yet.

"None of this makes any sense," Mom said. "Anyone reading this verse out loud will get a hole in their roof. That curses everyone."

Aunt Pearl shook her head. "Not true. The curse only works when it's recited by a witch. They were careful too, planting it in a newspaper that no one but Cen ever reads."

I scowled at her. "Who's 'they'?"

Silence.

"Plenty of people read my paper," I said defensively. "Aunt Pearl, somebody—tell me more about the curse. How can I possibly protect myself when I don't know what I'm up against?"

Aunt Pearl snapped, "I'll tell you later. Right now, we need to counter the curse before it causes insurmountable damage.

"You can't reverse something that doesn't exist," Mom said.

"Watch me." Aunt Pearl lifted her arms and spoke in a loud voice:

I BLAST your curse from the skies,
   I extinguish it before your eyes,
   You shall not burden us again,
   Go away with all your ken,
   I will guard and protect this place,

Do not dare to show your face,
Your witchy powers are no more,
Forever locked behind the door,
Forever changed from witch to mortal,
Eternally banished from the portal,
You will pay for your grave misdeeds,
All your dreams will die as seeds,
No more will your curses sprout,
For eternity, you shall live in doubt,
Forty years and a day,
Which time you shall stay away.

SHE LOWERED arms ad wiped one palm against another. "Done. Now we just have to wait and see."

Grandma Vi cleared her throat. "Now can I tell Cen about the Rocklins?"

"No. I should be the one to explain the Rocklin curse," Aunt Pearl insisted as she took a seat at the breakfast nook. She glared at Grandma Vi. "You were too directly involved to describe it accurately."

"Fine, have it your way." Grandma Vi flushed with anger.

Aunt Pearl said wistfully, "Our two witch families, the Wests and the Rocklins, lived in harmony for decades. We split our vortex duties, and even shared potions and spells. Everything worked great. Then one witch, Eliza Rocklin, developed an unquenchable thirst for power.

"Until that time, Westwick Corners was a supernatural utopia of sorts. We practised our spells openly, our magical herb gardens flourished, and we did as we pleased. Our only obligation was to guard the energy vortex. We had it so good, and we didn't even know it."

I frowned. "Mom, why didn't you tell me any of this?"

"I, uh, didn't think—"

Aunt Pearl cut her off. "Ruby was only twelve or thirteen at the time. She was just as self-absorbed back then as she is now. All she cared about was tending her herb garden and baking. I was the older, wiser sister. I was well aware of the consequences of slipping up. If we lost the vortex, we wouldn't be able to survive in this town. I'd end up waitressing at the Shady Creek Café. Can you even imagine?"

"Absolutely not." I shuddered at the thought of Aunt Pearl serving customers and expecting tips.

"Anyhow, Eliza was in her late twenties, a passable witch I guess, but not nearly as good as me. She was also quite manipulative. She thought that with some trickery, her family could control the vortex completely. She wanted to cut our family out of the picture. Sharing power wasn't enough for Eliza. She wanted to turn our vortex into a theme park."

I gasped. "Just like what we went through a few years ago with Tonya Plant?" What was it with witches and theme parks?

Aunt Pearl nodded. "Exactly. Except Eliza succeeded. For a period of time, she completely controlled the vortex."

"You let her do that?" It was hard to imagine Aunt Pearl allowing that to happen.

Aunt Pearl shrugged. "She was already a very powerful witch, Cen. I was still learning my craft."

I held up my hand. "You just said that you were the better witch."

"Quit arguing, Cendrine. Anyway, once Eliza disabled our powers, she shut down the energy vortex completely."

"How could she do that? I thought the vortex was stronger than any one being."

Aunt Pearl sighed. "I hope this doesn't take all day. Eliza was as devious as they come. She tricked us into disabling our powers, and then temporarily transferring our powers to her."

My mouth dropped open. I couldn't imagine Aunt Pearl handing over power—or taking orders from anyone. "Why would you do that?"

"Eliza convinced us that something terrible would happen to the vortex if we didn't. A power transfer is reserved for the direst of circumstances. Eliza convinced your Grandma that the power transfer was necessary to recalibrate the vortex. Something about the energy field being off and our powers interfering with it. Nothing I ever would have believed but—"

Grandma Vi interrupted. "You would have done the same thing in my position and you know it, Pearl."

Mom said, "It's all in the past, but once Eliza disabled our powers, she cast a spell to freeze our powers indefinitely. She planned to seize the portal and operate it for profit."

"It's against WICCA rules to profit from spells," I said.

Aunt Pearl rolled her eyes. "Don't be so naïve, Cen. People break rules all the time. Eliza was a criminal witch out to steal from everyone else. And she succeeded."

"You hid all this from me?" My face flushed, hurt that my entire family had withheld such a significant part of our family history from me.

"You weren't quite ready for it before," Aunt Pearl snapped.

Unlike the curse, I knew plenty about the vortex. It was impossible not to know. Every witch felt the pull of the magnetic force whenever we came or went from Westwick Corners.

Our vortex wasn't known to the general public like Stonehenge or Sedona, Arizona. However, it was very well known in the supernatural world. Like all energy vortexes, it magnified one's supernatural powers and was a portal to other dimensions and worlds.

Powers diminished the further you moved from the vortex. Spellcasting always felt a tiny bit harder in Shady Creek, and whenever I left the state completely, I operated at about 75% of my normal strength. It was as invisible as a radio wave, and being out of range was like spellcasting on an almost-drained battery. Whenever I returned home or got closer to another energy vortex, my spellcasting recharged.

I frowned. "Eliza must have failed in the end, because our powers remain intact. How did you get them back?"

"We had to call in reinforcements," Grandma Vi added.

"You make it sound like a war."

"It was exactly that. A covert war, where we were attacked in secret." Grandma Vi looked sad. "No one believed us, and few would help us."

Mom changed the subject. "Maybe you ladies have time to chat all day, but I don't. I've got to get these flower arrangements over to Serena. I also need to shop for tonight's dinner, check in on our upstairs guests, and get ready for tomorrow's breakfast. It's called earning a living."

"What can I do?" I asked.

But Mom didn't hear. She was already in the hallway, slipping into her coat.

We were shadows of our former selves. Aunt Pearl was afraid. Mom was short-tempered. And I was suddenly uncertain about everything. Something had changed in all of us, and I felt powerless to stop it.

CHAPTER 10

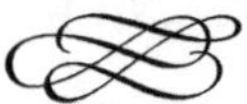

I finally finished my Valentine's Day article and headed outside. Jason's Porsche was still parked in the lot by The Witching Post. I considered waiting until later to ask Lucky about the photographer gig but decided it couldn't wait. We didn't have much time to organize Steve and Serena's vow renewal ceremony. Given Lucky's frequent absences, this could be my last chance.

I opened the bar door and walked inside, pausing as Lucky's and Jason's voices drifted toward me from the bar. The two men continued talking, unaware of my presence.

"I can make anything happen. All it takes is money." Lucky wiped down the bar and removed Jason's empty beer bottle.

"How much?" Jason pulled out his wallet from his back pocket.

Lucky scratched his chin. "It depends…but based on what you said I can probably get it done for ten grand."

"Hmm…okay. How soon?"

Lucky opened another bottle of beer and placed it on the bar in front of Jason. "Soon as you pay me. I'll get things started."

As I listened to their sketchy-sounding conversation, I flashed back to Lucky's resume when we hired him. There were large, unexplained gaps in his employment history, but the few jobs listed were mostly at bars and fast-food restaurants. Criminal for hire hadn't been one of them.

I walked over to the bar and pulled out a barstool, loudly dragging the chair on the floor to announce myself. I sat down a few stools away from Jason.

Lucky seemed startled by my presence. "Oh—hi, Cendrine. Can I get you a drink?"

"Uh, no thanks, Lucky. I'm here to ask you something. Can we talk in private?" I asked.

"No need. I was just leaving." Jason scowled and rose from his seat. He turned to Lucky. "I'll call you later."

I waited until Jason was out the door and I heard the Porsche engine revving in the parking lot. "Lucky, I need your help. A couple of our guests are renewing their vows, and I need a photographer for tomorrow. Are you interested? It's pretty straightforward. Take a few shots of the ceremony before and after, nothing fancy. It's a few hours at the most."

Lucky raised his hands and shrugged. "Me? Take wedding pictures? I don't even own a camera."

"That's okay. I'll provide the camera. I'll even drive you there and back myself. It pays triple your bartending rate." I hoped it was an offer he couldn't refuse.

He raised his brows. "Oh really? Well, it just so happens

that I'm in desperate need of some quick cash. My rent is overdue, and I already spent the money."

"Great," I said. "The ceremony is around noon, but I still need to confirm the time. Just show up here for your shift as usual, and we'll drive over. I'll get someone to cover for you while you're gone." If Aunt Pearl wouldn't agree to cover for Lucky, then I would close the bar as a last resort.

"Deal." Lucky flashed his million-dollar smile. "Can't wait."

CHAPTER 11

I returned to the inn to work on my story. I sat at the breakfast nook, my stomach growling as I stole glances at the big bowl of muffins on the kitchen island. I was halfway through writing the first draft of my Real McCoys article. Then Mom called, and everything changed.

She sobbed hysterically. Her wails were so loud that I had to hold my phone away from my ear. Her speech came in short gasps, so disjointed that it was hard to make out her words.

"I'm at the Rocklin place. There's been an, uh—terrible accident!" Mom cried. "Come quick!"

"An accident? What happened?" I turned up the volume on my phone.

Aunt Pearl, who stood nearby, heard everything, and her eyes widened in fear. "It's that darn curse!"

I held my hand up for quiet so I could decipher Mom's incoherent speech.

Mom's words tumbled out in short bursts. "I j-just found Steve McCoy. He was floating in the pool, face down. I think he's—d-d-dead. I don't know what to—"

Aunt Pearl grabbed the phone from my hand and shouted into it. "Do you believe me now, Ruby? Get out of there! We're doomed!"

I snatched my phone back. Mom's confused, broken sentences were hard to understand, especially with the new, strange clicking noise on the line. "Mom, slow down and tell me what happened. You're not making any sense."

She spoke haltingly between sobs. "I-I-tried to save him. I jumped into the water, tried to…to move…him…but it was…too late. I think he's d-d-dead."

The clicking sound, I now realized, was Mom's chattering teeth. She had jumped into the pool, fully clothed, in sub-zero temperature.

"I'll be right there, Mom. Just stay on the line, and don't do anything more till I get there."

She was probably already hypothermic, or worse. I ran into the hallway and slipped on my coat and shoes. I grabbed Mom's heaviest winter coat from the hall closet and headed outside.

I half-walked, half-ran to my car in the parking lot, talking as I went. "Did you call the fire department?" Westwick Corners wasn't big enough to have 9-1-1 emergency dispatch or even paramedics. Everything was handled by the volunteer fire department. If we needed additional assistance, we requested help from Shady Creek, a larger town more than an hour away. Needless to say, in the event we needed their help, it was probably already too late.

"I-I called you first. What should I do?" Mom's speech was becoming slurred and harder to understand by the minute. Mom should have called Sheriff Tyler Gates first, but she was too panicked to think straight.

I opened the front door and ran outside to my car, Mom's heavy coat draped over my shoulder. "I'll call for help. Just try to stay warm until we get there."

Aunt Pearl ran up behind me just as I opened the car door. She grabbed Mom's coat off my shoulder, squeezed my wrist and cried, "You can't go there, Cendrine! You'll never make it out alive."

I wrestled my arm from her surprisingly strong grip and climbed into the drivers' seat. I called Tyler.

Aunt Pearl swore under her breath and ran around to the passenger side of the SUV. She pulled on the door handle and scrambled into the passenger seat. She tossed Mom's coat into the backseat. "You're not going. I forbid it."

"Of course, I'm going. Mom needs help."

Tyler answered his phone right away.

I explained Mom's tragic discovery as I started the car and put it into gear. "Mom's at the Rocklin Mansion. She found a man floating in the pool. Unresponsive."

"Hold on, I'll dispatch the firefighters." I heard static as Tyler talked on his handheld radio and a male voice in the background said something indecipherable. "Okay, they're on their way over there. Why is Ruby even at the Rocklin place? I thought it was abandoned."

"Mom leased the place and she's rented it to some out-of-town guests. You've probably heard of them. It's the Real

McCoys, the family from that reality TV show. I think Mom's there alone, but she was really hard to understand. She said she found Steve McCoy floating in the pool." A vision of Mom struggling to pull Steve, a man twice her size, across the pool flashed through my mind.

Tyler said, "I'm headed there right now."

"Me too." I ended the call and glanced across the inn's parking lot to the empty space where Jason's car had been parked earlier. Had he returned to the Rocklin Mansion? Mom hadn't mentioned anyone else being present. There wasn't a whole lot for an angry young man to do around town though. A few minutes in either direction led to only fields, orchards, and vineyards in winter dormancy.

Jason would have some explaining to do, especially if Steve's death turned out to be more than just a horrible accident. I flashed back to their earlier argument. How far would an entitled, arrogant son go to get his way?

If Jason was innocent and didn't know about his father yet, he soon would. So would the world. A celebrity, drowned in a pool in an almost-ghost town, far away from Hollywood. Westwick Corners was about to be discovered. And not in a good way.

I glanced sideways at Aunt Pearl. "You said never go near the Rocklin place, that it's too dangerous. Why are you even here?"

"One dead body is one too many. Desperate times call for desperate magic, Cen. We'll need to cast spells that are far, far beyond your capabilities."

"I'm perfectly capable of taking care of things." Realistically, all I could manage was keeping Aunt Pearl away from our guests at the best of times. Counteracting a curse at a potential crime scene was almost certainly beyond my abilities. But having Aunt Pearl there would undoubtedly make things worse.

I drove down our long, winding gravel driveway as fast as possible without losing control. Gravel sprayed as I turned onto the road and accelerated.

"You'll blow this, Cendrine. Between you and your mother—"

"You really should have stayed at the inn, Aunt Pearl. Lucky needs supervision, in case you haven't noticed."

"Don't you dare try to get rid of me. You need my help more than ever. Ruby got us into this mess and you helped her. As usual, I'm the only one who can get us out of it."

Arguing with Aunt Pearl was pointless. I glanced over and saw my phone in her hand.

Her head was bent forward as she whispered into the phone in a low voice.

"Who are you talking to?" I soon realized the phone was merely a prop to hide what she was really doing: spell-casting.

Aunt Pearl clutched a handful of polished rocks in her left hand and muttered in a low voice.

"Aunt Pearl, stop! You're making things worse."

"Things can't get any worse, Cendrine. We've got to fight this curse with everything we've got. Steve was the first victim, but he won't be the last."

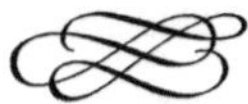

CHAPTER 12

We arrived at the Rocklin Mansion to find the Westwick Corners Fire Engine No. 1 truck had already arrived. It was parked at an angle in the driveway near the side of the house. Tyler's Jeep was there too, parked in the circular drive, in front of the house. I steered my SUV to the far end of the driveway and parked, out of the way of emergency vehicles. The wheels had barely stopped turning when Aunt Pearl jumped from the passenger seat and slammed the door. The winter sun glinted off her purple-sequined tracksuit as she ran across the driveway toward Tyler's Jeep.

I drew in my breath, fearing the worst as I climbed out of the driver's seat and reached into the backseat for Mom's coat. I slammed the car door and hurried after Aunt Pearl. As I ran, male voices drifted from behind the tall laurel hedge that separated the front yard from the side yard and pool. Probably the firefighters, frantically working to revive Steve.

Tyler exited his Jeep, talking on his cell phone. He was out of uniform, casually dressed in a flannel shirt, jeans, and hiking boots. He paused with his jacket in hand before placing it back inside the Jeep. Our eyes met momentarily before he turned to Aunt Pearl, who had reached him with a speed of an Olympic sprinter.

She was half Tyler's size, but she grabbed his arm with so much force that his phone flew out of his hand as he staggered backward.

She half-shouted at him. "You better get a handle on this quick, sheriff. More deaths are about to follow."

Tyler bent to pick up his phone. He rose and turned to Aunt Pearl. "This better be good. You got some inside information you want to share, Pearl?"

"Where's Ruby, Sheriff?" Aunt Pearl scanned the grounds.

Tyler walked calmly over to the Jeep and opened the passenger door. "She's sitting right here."

Mom lifted her head, which had been bent forward and gave a weak wave. She was crying.

Aunt Pearl ran over to Mom and pulled her from the Jeep. "I need to check you over, Ruby, to make sure you're undamaged."

I helped Mom into her coat, just as two volunteer firefighters emerged from the side of the house and walked slowly toward the fire truck. Their lack of urgency meant only one thing. Steve was already dead.

I cleared my throat. "Is Steve McCoy really—?"

The men cast their eyes downward, avoiding my gaze.

"He's gone," the older one said.

Tyler touched my arm. "The Medical Examiner is on her way over right now."

The ME was an hour away in Shady Creek, and my call notifying Tyler had been only a few minutes ago. It would be a while before she arrived on scene. Dread formed in the pit of my stomach as I watched the firefighters slowly put away their gear. Maybe Grandma Vi and Aunt Pearl were right about the Rocklin curse. The odds of drowning in an outdoor pool in the dead of winter were extremely low.

On the other hand, swimming in such conditions was highly unusual. Steve had mentioned his plans to swim in the outdoor pool earlier, despite the frigid temperatures. That indicated that he had gone to the pool voluntarily, and dramatic temperature shifts could trigger a heart attack or other health issue in even the healthiest people. I had a hard time dipping a toe into an indoor heated pool and couldn't imagine a workout consisting of plunging into ice-cold water in the dead of winter.

Still, I couldn't shake off my suspicion of foul play. Something wasn't right, though I couldn't quite put my finger on it.

Westwick Corners would now be forever known as the place where one-half of The Real McCoys met an untimely death. While Steve McCoy wasn't the first dead vacationer in our town, he would probably be the last. No one was likely to visit once the news was out. On a per capita basis for tourists, our mortality rate was awfully high.

The West family business, and the town's tourism business, built up so painstakingly over the years, were doomed. On the other hand, reality shows were proof that even bad news brought name recognition, and notoriety was better than obscurity.

Tyler touched my shoulder and motioned to a spot a few feet away and out of earshot. He cleared his throat. "Ruby hasn't been making any sense. She said she owns this place. Since when, Cen? She never mentioned it before."

My face flushed as I debated how little or how much I should tell him. "Uh…she um…got it recently. I can't remember the exact date."

"You never mentioned—"

I cut him off with a raised hand. "She only told us this morning."

Tyler raised his brows at my abruptness. "Ruby always says the inn's finances are tight. This place must have cost a fortune. How could she afford it?"

I bit my lip as I struggled with how much to reveal of Mom's project. "Mom said she got a great deal, and that she did a lot to fix it up. She didn't want to tell us because Aunt Pearl insists that the place is cursed." Tyler knew we were witches, but getting into the curse details didn't seem right. He also knew nothing about Grandma Vi, so I left her out. Living with a ghost grandma defied logic, and Tyler had plenty else to focus on right now.

Tyler nodded. "Who in their right mind swims in sub-zero temperatures in the dead of winter? An accidental drowning in an outdoor pool in February seems a bit far-fetched. For once I agree with Pearl. This place probably is cursed."

After I recounted Steve's mention of swimming, I looked around for Aunt Pearl, but she had vanished, along with

Mom. I turned back to Tyler. "Is it okay for them just to walk around unsupervised?"

"Absolutely not. They must have gone over to the pool." He motioned for me to follow.

"You don't think it was an accident, do you? Steve told Mom and me that he swam every day."

Tyler shrugged. "It's too early to determine that. Why do you suspect something other than an accident? Do you know something I don't?"

I briefly recounted the McCoys' earlier argument, and what I had overheard between Lucky and Jason at the bar. "I'm not sure, really. The McCoys said they chose Westwick Corners because it's off the beaten track. They claimed their trip was a secret."

"That limits the suspect pool if it checks out. It also makes for fewer witnesses to murder, if that's what you're getting at," Tyler said.

I frowned. "Big stars like the McCoys probably have crazy fans too, maybe even stalkers. Even if the McCoys didn't tell anyone about their secret getaway, somebody could have followed them here to Westwick Corners. Oh, and one more thing. The Real McCoys have a small crew here. They just checked into the inn this morning."

Tyler scratched his chin thoughtfully. "They're filming here?"

"Steve and Serena called it a holiday, but you know how reality shows work. They film and monetize every waking moment. Maybe a disgruntled crew member had it in for Steve?"

"You've already decided it's murder, Cen, but you're jumping to conclusions. The medical examiner isn't even here yet to examine the body. Why would one of the crew kill one half of the reality show that gave them a paycheck? If the show goes on hiatus, they're out of a job."

"I-I uh, just have this feeling."

We paused at the gate, which had been re-latched.

Tyler lifted the latch and opened the gate, which was securely bolted to the side to the house and bordered by a four-foot-high laurel hedge on the other side. The hedge's height allowed privacy while swimming or sunbathing but also allowed anyone standing directly inside or outside the hedge a view of both the front and back yard.

"Pearl has you all worked up," he said as we walked through the gate to see Mom and Aunt Pearl standing by the hedge just inside the pool gate. He pointed at them. "Don't either of you move again unless I say so."

Mom nodded apologetically but Aunt Pearl was unresponsive. She swayed on her feet, trancelike, speaking in a low voice. I couldn't make out the words despite being only a few feet away. I didn't need to hear them, because I recognized the cadence of a magic spell. It was far too late for any protection spell, but Aunt Pearl probably figured that it was worth a shot. She repeated the spell three times, but her words had no effect.

She stomped her foot like a child having a temper tantrum. "Oh, for crying out loud! See what you've done, Ruby? My powers have totally evaporated, just like that." Aunt Pearl snapped her fingers, but they made no sound. "My fingers don't even snap anymore."

Tyler sighed, clearly frustrated. "Cen, let's get them back out front. Whatever you do, don't look—"

It was too late; I had already turned to look. My eyes

locked on a stretcher beside the pool. It was completely covered with a plastic sheet, but there was no mistaking the contours of a body underneath. I gasped.

Tyler wrapped an arm around my shoulder and turned me around. "We're going to leave the scene now so that nothing is disturbed."

Aunt Pearl, out of her trance, swore. "We're ruined! Every single one of us!"

I whispered to Tyler, "Aunt Pearl thinks Steve's death is a result of a curse against our family. I wish there was a more logical explanation to get her off all of this curse business. I'm afraid she'll do something extreme."

"Your logical explanation seems to have jumped straight to murder," Tyler said. "It could simply be a tragic accident."

"Maybe, but you'll investigate all angles, right?" If it was an accident, Aunt Pearl would blame the curse. If it was murder, and the killer was caught, then there would be another explanation for Steve's tragic ending.

"Of course, I will. I've got to consider every possibility. If it was foul play—and I'm not saying I think it is—then this was likely personal. A small town, away from prying eyes. Somebody wanting to get away with murder…"

My thoughts drifted back to Jason. His car was gone from the Witching Post when I left. He was mad at Steve and Serena, and his conversation with Lucky had sounded suspicious. Jason was angry and entitled, but was he capable of murdering his father?

"C'mon. Let's all go sit in my Jeep while we wait for the Shady Creek police and medical examiner." Tyler motioned for all of us to follow him. Mom got into the Jeep's front passenger seat. I climbed into the backseat after Aunt Pearl who had already grabbed Tyler's jacket sitting on the seat. Her teeth chattered as she put on Tyler's too-big jacket and shoved her hands in the pockets.

Tyler cranked the heat up full blast and turned sideways in his seat to face Mom in the passenger seat. "Ruby, start from the beginning. What happened?"

Mom's teeth chattered as she spoke. "I came to drop off some flower arrangement ideas for Serena to look at. And I had some other wedding ideas to discuss. Steven and Serena are renewing their vows, you know." She looked pointedly at Tyler and glanced at me in the rear-view mirror.

I rolled my eyes at Mom's obvious marriage hint. I thought it was inappropriate and tacky, considering the grave circumstances that had brought us here.

Tyler, apparently oblivious to Mom's cue, said, "Okay, so what happened next?"

"Steve invited me inside. He said Serena was out shopping and that he was about to go for a swim. He told me to drop off the floral arrangement ideas in the kitchen, which I did. I scribbled a note for Serena, and I shut off the hot water tap in the kitchen that was dripping. Then I headed out. But as I was leaving, I remembered that I also needed to confirm the menu. I called out again for Steve. When he didn't answer, I went outside to the pool to look for him. That's when I found him." Mom burst into tears.

"How long were you there before you started to leave?" Tyler asked.

Mom's lower lip trembled. "Only about five minutes. I still can't believe that one minute he was alive, and then—"

"It only takes seconds to drown." Aunt Pearl pulled her

closed fist out of Tyler's jacket. She opened her palm to reveal a ring box.

My eyes widened in horror. I whispered, "Put it back!"

Aunt Pearl smirked. She put her hand back in the jacket pocket, but then pulled it out again. This time she opened the ring box to reveal a beautiful diamond solitaire ring. Just as quickly she snapped the box closed.

I gasped. Luckily, Tyler was focused on Mom and didn't notice what was going on in the backseat.

Mom's words were broken by sobs. "I-I did all I could do —I jumped into the pool to pull Steve to safety. I grabbed his arm and tried to pull him to the side of the pool, but the water was so cold that my hands froze. I tried to do CPR, but in the middle of the pool it just wouldn't work. I tried my hardest, but he's a big man. He was just too heavy to pull out of the pool."

I stated the obvious. "You could have used a spell."

Mom sighed. "I tried that first, but nothing happened. All my powers have vanished."

Tyler frowned. "Did you call for help?"

"Yes," Mom whispered. "In fact, I screamed but one answered. I didn't see or hear anyone else. I was all alone."

"I warned you." Aunt Pearl elbowed me in the ribs.

"Hey!" I leaned forward, wincing in pain. I had done nothing to deserve such punishment, but apparently, I was the next best target after Mom, safely out of reach in the front seat.

Aunt Pearl shoved me. "Believe me now, Cen? We never should have set foot on this property. If we leave now, maybe it's not too late to undo Ruby's actions and get our powers back."

As I shifted away from Aunt Pearl, the waist button on my pants snapped off. I was gaining more weight by the minute.

Aunt Pearl snickered. "Fatso."

I swore under my breath.

"Nobody's going anywhere until I say so." Tyler pressed the Jeep's door lock button as if to underline his point.

Mom's money-making scheme was literally cursed. So, apparently, was I. Aunt Pearl had stolen Tyler's engagement ring and seemed hell-bent on sabotaging his proposal. Things were quickly progressing from bad to worse. We were powerless as witches, and the only thing growing was my waistline.

What more could possibly go wrong?

CHAPTER 13

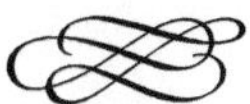

After Mom recounted the sequence of events several times, Tyler asked her to return with him to the pool. Mom hesitated, insistent that Aunt Pearl and I accompany her. Tyler made Aunt Pearl and I both promise that we wouldn't touch anything. We trailed behind Tyler and Mom as they walked ahead of us and through the side gate that led to the pool area.

Our presence at the scene of a death was completely unorthodox, but so was the strange transformation happening to Mom. Her speech grew incoherent, and she stumbled as she walked. Tyler needed Mom's eyewitness account while the events were fresh in her mind, yes, but he also required our assistance, given Mom's ever-worsening condition.

Mom grew more and more agitated by the minute, egged on by Aunt Pearl's accusations of awakening the curse. I tried to stop Aunt Pearl from making things worse than they already were, but she was hell-bent on extracting an apology from Mom.

Tyler motioned for Aunt Pearl and me to stay by the gate as he walked with Mom toward the pool. He turned back and held up his hand. "Don't move, and please don't look at anything."

Of course, looking was the first thing we did, as soon as Tyler's back was turned. I followed behind Aunt Pearl. She looked ridiculous wearing Tyler's jacket which was about ten sizes too large for her. She had rolled up the sleeves, but the jacket hem almost reached her knees.

Mom's muffin basket was overturned near the edge of the pool. A trail of muffins led to the pool, where at least three floated like little islands on the steaming water.

Aunt Pearl grabbed my wrist in a painful vice-like grip. "Kind of makes you lose your appetite, doesn't it, Cen?"

"Ouch!" I snatched my arm away just as I caught a flash of movement by my side. I outstretched my arm to grab Aunt Pearl, but it was too late. Within seconds she was by the pool.

"Get back here!" I kept my voice to a loud whisper, just enough for her to hear.

She ignored me.

Tyler and Mom had already moved toward the French doors that led into the house, their backs turned. They were deep in conversation, unaware of Aunt Pearl's actions.

I ran toward the pool and whispered loudly, "Aunt Pearl, get away from the pool!"

Tyler and Mom were completely oblivious to Aunt

Pearl's transgression. Mom retraced her steps as she recounted her timeline of events.

Aunt Pearl continued to ignore me as she knelt by the pool. She dipped her hand into the pool, wetting the sleeve of Tyler's jacket. Inside her cupped hand was the engagement ring.

"What are you doing?" I hissed.

She rose unsteadily to her feet, almost losing her balance before steadying herself. She opened her hand and placed the engagement ring between her index finger and thumb. She held it up to the light and squinted. "I wonder if it's real?"

"Of course, it's real. Put it back!" I ran toward her and grabbed her other hand. I pulled her from the pool edge. "Get away from the pool or I'll—"

"You'll do what, Cendrine? You're totally out of your element here and so is the sheriff. We're dealing with a deadly curse, and your boyfriend isn't equipped to deal with it." She yanked her hand from mine and knelt again by the pool edge. She reached her arm into the water and stirred it up with a cupped hand to create a current to bring the floating muffins closer.

I gasped. "Aunt Pearl! You're close enough to fall in."

As if on cue, Aunt Pearl teetered dangerously at the edge.

"Get away from there!"

"I-I have to remove our traces—"

"What traces?" I lunged toward her and grabbed her left arm and pulled her away. She tumbled behind me, landing a few feet safely away from the pool. Unfortunately, that caused me to lose my balance as well. I fell forward onto the patio and as I did, my right hand dipped into the pool.

"Cendrine! You've contaminated the scene!" Aunt Pearl was already on her feet, surprisingly agile. She rubbed her hands together to shake off the frost from the pool deck.

Her hands were empty. There was no sign of the engagement ring.

"Where's the ring? Is it back in your pocket?" I was still on the ground, finding it hard to push myself up due to my ever-expanding girth and the icy cement.

Aunt Pearl sniffed. "It's taken care of. I did what I needed to save us. In order to do that, I need to remove all traces so that the Rocklins don't—"

I gasped. "The ring has nothing to do with that. Where is it?"

"Hey, get away from there!" Tyler hurried over, a frustrated expression on his face. Mom shuffled behind him, her teeth chattering.

I rolled backwards onto my butt and immediately felt the frigid cement sear through my clothes. I pressed myself up into a sitting position and shook the water off my hand, which already tingled from the icy cold. I had expected more warmth from a heated pool, even an outdoor pool on a cold February day. I forced my now-numb butt off the frozen concrete and pushed myself up to a standing position. Steve was crazy to swim in this weather.

Tyler reached his hand down and helped me up. "What happened?"

"Aunt Pearl was about to—"

She smirked, her arms crossed. "I told Cen to stay by the gate, but she wouldn't listen. She slipped on the icy concrete and lost her balance. Luckily, I stopped her from falling into the water before she ended up like that guy." She pointed at the stretcher.

I glared at her.

"I can't leave you two alone for a second without a catastrophe." Tyler pointed to the gate. "Pearl, take Ruby to Cen's car and get her warmed up. Cendrine, you come with me."

I grabbed Aunt Pearl's arm and whispered, "The ring is in your pocket, right?"

"Probably."

"Can you at least check?" I felt sick at the thought of the ring lying at the bottom of the pool. Had the ring been in Tyler's jacket all along? Or had Aunt Pearl found the ring in his Jeep somehow? I didn't think she would do something that drastic, but I also couldn't imagine Tyler being so careless as to leave an expensive diamond ring in his jacket.

There was nothing more I could do or say in front of Tyler since I wasn't even supposed to know about the ring. Instead, I tossed Aunt Pearl my keys. "Crank the heat. There's a blanket and some extra clothes in the trunk."

Aunt Pearl placed her hands on her hips. "Why does Cendrine get to stay—"

"Just go." Tyler cut her off. He waited until Aunt Pearl was on the other side of the gate and turned to me. "What the heck was that all about?"

"I-I'm sorry. All of a sudden Aunt Pearl was by the pool. She lost her balance and I thought she was going to fall in, so I grabbed her. I lost my balance instead." I looked down, embarrassed. My butt had even left a mark on the frosty pool deck.

Tyler rubbed his forehead. "She's trouble wherever she goes. I should have been watching myself. Something…I don't remember what…distracted me. It's weird…I don't feel quite right."

"I'm not feeling so great either." My thoughts kept drifting, and I had trouble concentrating on the present. Everything seemed hazy like a daydream, albeit a nightmarish one. Maybe the curse was real after all.

"Hey!" A man's voice boomed behind us.

I spun around to see Lucky standing at the gate.

I hurried toward him and blocked his path forward. "You can't come any further. Why are you here? You're supposed to be bartending at The Witching Post."

Lucky frowned. "No, you told me to come here, to take pictures. I waited at the bar for over an hour, Cen. You forgot to pick me up."

"That assignment was for tomorrow, not today." Not only did Lucky have the wrong time and day, but I was pretty sure I hadn't given Lucky any specifics. I certainly hadn't given him the address, since I had planned to drive him. I had never mentioned the ceremony was taking place at the Rocklin place. Jason could have told him, except that Jason didn't know about the vow renewals either. According to Steve and Serena, Mom and I were the only ones in on the secret. "Who's tending bar?"

"Pearl, I guess. I'm positive you said it was today."

I took a deep breath to calm myself. Lucky had screwed up the simplest of instructions that I had given him less than an hour ago: One p.m. tomorrow at the Witching Post, to be confirmed first. Was he really this dumb, or was there something else going on? I flashed back to the conversation I had overheard earlier between Lucky and Jason at the bar. I couldn't be sure of course, but it had sounded almost criminal. Was Lucky's presence more sinister than just a mistake?

"No, I definitely said tomorrow. Pearl's been with me the whole time so you couldn't have heard it from her. Did you even lock the bar before you left?"

Lucky was silent. He turned and looked off into the distance, avoiding eye contact. His sullen expression told me that he hadn't done either of those things. Mom was right. Hiring him had been a costly mistake.

I said, "There's been a change of plans and we don't need a photographer after all." I glanced back at the hedge surrounding the pool. With one half of the couple dead, it was a pretty safe bet that the wedding vow renewal wasn't going to happen.

"You sure it wasn't today?"

He just wanted to be right.

"I'm sure, Lucky. I was going to drive you, remember? Doesn't matter. The ceremony is canceled."

I glanced out at the parking lot, but there was no sign of Lucky's Ford truck. How he had traveled to the mansion without a vehicle, and without me providing an address to him, was a mystery.

I was so infuriated with Lucky that I was tempted to place a spell on him. A spell had the side benefit of proving or disproving Mom's claim that her spells had been disabled when she tried to rescue Steve. But that seemed unethical, so I decided against it.

Lucky looked beyond me toward the pool. Then he turned to look back at the fire trucks and Tyler's Jeep in the parking lot. He turned back and pointed at the stretcher. "That the dude who was getting married? Looks like he got cold feet."

CHAPTER 14

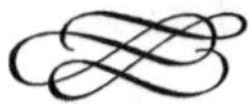

The next few hours were a blur. Aunt Pearl drove Lucky home in my Honda SUV. The Shady Creek Medical Examiner and the Shady Creek Police arrived soon after. The ME's preliminary determination was that Steven McCoy's cause of death appeared to be drowning, but that still needed confirmation. An autopsy would confirm whether water was present in his lungs, which would indicate that he had been alive when he entered the water. His manner of death, whether accidental, homicide, or something else, was still an unknown. That would be confirmed only once the autopsy was done. Determining the manner of death could be quite complex. The presence or absence of other injuries, as well as evidence at the scene, would all require analysis and assessment.

Given the unusual circumstances, the Shady Creek

crime scene techs were called out and worked the scene, a precautionary evidence-gathering operation to definitively rule out—or rule in—foul play. Was Steve's death a tragic accident, murder, or was there another cause, like the Rocklin curse?

I stood by the pool gate, shivering from my frozen, sore butt. I anxiously watched from a distance. I held a faint hope that if an engagement ring had really fallen into the pool, the police would surely find it. The alternative of it being gone forever was also a possibility. The idea filled me with dread. I inhaled the frigid air and tried to calm myself as I waited for Tyler to finish talking with the Shady Creek CSI techs. They seemed to be packing up with no apparent 'ah ha' moment of finding a diamond ring. The ME had already removed Steve's body and it was enroute to Shady Creek for autopsy.

I wasn't convinced that Steve's death had been an accident. I didn't believe it was the Rocklin curse, either. Each of those outcomes seemed wrong, but with my thoughts still scattered, I couldn't quite figure out why I thought that way. I wasn't ready to share my concerns with Tyler just yet.

Aside from the obvious quirk of Steve wanting to swim outside on a frigid February day, there were other things that troubled me. The patio was still covered with a thin layer of frost from the previous night. My bum print was still visible on the pavement, as were the footprints from the police, which were confined to a clearly marked path. I now realized that, prior to their arrival, there had been no other footprints around the pool—including no footprints that could have been made by Steve. The only visible prints were Mom's, obvious because of her small feet as well as the distinctive tread on the soles of her clogs.

Steve was fit, but he was still a big man, heavy enough to have made marks on the frost-covered concrete. His tracks should have remained visible for hours. Yet Mom and I talked to him inside the house just a few hours earlier. Then Mom had seen him again, just minutes before she found him floating in the pool. If he hadn't walked to the pool, then how had he gotten there?

Someone could have carried him there. That seemed unlikely since it would have taken two strong men to carry him. Yet, according to Mom, she hadn't seen or heard anyone else at the house.

The back door had been closed but unlocked, but a thorough search of the mansion by the Shady Creek police had found no one else home. Jason had argued with Steve. How much earlier had Jason left the Witching Post parking lot before I had noticed his car gone? Jason's departure around the time of Steve's death raised the possibility that he could be involved. Where had Jason gone after leaving the Witching Post? The only places open were the general store, a women's clothing store, and a café, places unlikely to appeal to a guy like Jason. Or maybe he had just gone for a drive. In any case, he had no alibi.

I flashed back to Jason's odd conversation with Lucky. Had he told Lucky where Steve and Serena were staying? If so, why had he revealed the McCoys' top secret location to a stranger? Lucky's claim of confused dates sounded lame. Was it a hastily thought up lie to explain his presence at the mansion—and the scene of the crime? Lucky had no alibi either and even more importantly, no reason to be there.

My thoughts were broken by tires crunching on gravel. I turned around to see a white Mercedes SUV come up the drive and then disappear from view as it turned into the circular driveway in front of the house.

I walked over to Tyler and touched his arm to alert him. I whispered, "Serena McCoy, Steve's wife, has just arrived."

CHAPTER 15

Serena climbed out from the backseat of the Mercedes. She strode across the driveway to where Tyler and I waited just outside the gate to the pool. She had changed from her earlier casual wear into embroidered designer jeans and calf-height leather boots. A white angora sweater peeked out from under a calf-length fox fur coat. She was always perfectly put together whether on-camera or off, but that was about to fall apart.

She waved her hand at the police and fire vehicles parked out front, a confused expression on her face. "What's going on? Why are all these vehicles here?"

"This is Serena McCoy, Tyler." It sounded lame introducing a world-famous celebrity. Everyone knew who Serena was, including Tyler. She needed no introduction.

Tyler cleared his throat. "Mrs. McCoy, I'm afraid I have bad news."

Serena spun around, looking for anything amiss. Seeing nothing obvious, she crossed her arms and swore under her breath. "What has Jason gone and done now? That kid is so entitled. I'll pay to get it fixed, just don't tell—"

"It's not Jason, ma'am." Tyler kept his voice flat. "Let's go inside and I'll explain."

Serena nodded. "Does Steve know yet?"

"That's what I need to talk to you about, Mrs. McCoy." Tyler took her arm. "There's been an accident. Your husband is deceased."

* * *

HOURS LATER, after a quick trip home to change into dry clothes, Mom and I returned to the Rocklin mansion. According to Tyler, Serena had insisted on our presence.

The Shady Creek police had, at Tyler's request, examined the property, collected relevant evidence, and cleared the house. As the lone law enforcement in town, Tyler relied heavily on the forensics and investigation resources from the larger town. But the actual investigation and its conclusions were ultimately Tyler's responsibility.

Since the McCoys' arrival had been so recent, there hadn't been much to examine, according to the Shady Creek police on scene. Still, it seemed that the turnaround was incredibly fast for what was an unusual death, no matter what the cause. Had the police been rushed or else pressured by a high-profile death? Whatever the reason, it didn't inspire a lot of confidence.

Mom and I entered the mansion and paused in the living room doorway. The spacious, elegant living room now felt cavernous and cold, despite the roaring fire that Abby, Serena's assistant, had started.

Tyler motioned for us to sit beside him on one of two oversized burgundy sofas. Mom sat next to Tyler and I beside Mom. Serena and Abby sat across from us on a matching sofa. In the middle was a massive square mahogany coffee table, carved with the same intertwined rose and leaf motif as the fireplace mantel and other wood accents throughout the house.

Abby's arm was protectively draped around Serena's shoulder like a supportive friend rather than the employee she was. Serena's tear-streaked face was flushed a deep crimson. She rocked back and forth and stared down into her lap, avoiding eye contact and looking totally broken. I clenched the sofa's velvet armrest, feeling awkward and wishing I was someplace else.

The friendly vibe from our initial meeting had evaporated, replaced by a mood that was both sad and adversarial. It was highly unusual for Mom and me to be present while Tyler delivered bad news to a victim's spouse, but Serena had insisted that we be present. How could we refuse? I shuddered at the headlines that would probably be written about the 'death do us part' doomed vow renewal ceremony. It would almost certainly be written into the show since Steve's death couldn't go unexplained or unacknowledged. It was a reality show after all, and one of the two stars was suddenly dead. His story would be told no matter what. I didn't see any crew, but I still felt on edge. Were hidden cameras recording us right now? Maybe I was just being paranoid.

Tyler had reluctantly agreed to Serena's request for our

presence. He gave us strict instructions not to comment or answer any questions. Our job was to sit quietly. So we did our best to be silent sofa-sitting stage props. I hoped that our cooperation would keep Mom, and Westwick Corners in general, from any blame or lawsuits.

Serena slumped into the opposite sofa, a dazed expression on her tearstained face. "No, no, no! He can't be—" She wailed and buried her head in her hands.

"Serena is still not in any condition to talk," Abby said. "Can we reschedule for later?"

Tyler shook his head. "No. It's got to be now."

Abby's eyes flashed with anger at being shut down.

Tyler glanced at Serena, who wearily nodded her consent.

Serena said, "I want Abby to stay. She's my confidential assistant. Anything I know, she knows. I tell her anything and everything. Tell me again what happened."

Tyler drew a deep breath. "Ruby dropped by with flower arrangement samples. Steven told Ruby to drop them off in the kitchen. But when she called out for him a moment later and got no answer, she found him unresponsive in the pool."

"I still can't believe he drowned. Such a terrible, tragic accident!" Abby shook her head.

"It appears to be drowning, but we can't say for sure yet," Tyler said. "The medical examiner will confirm once she performs the autopsy."

"I'm so sorry, Serena. If there's anything more that we can do…" Mom's voice trailed off.

I patted Mom's hand and whispered, "We're not supposed to talk, remember?"

Mom grasped my hand in return and didn't say anything more.

Abby rose to her feet and turned to Serena. "I'll call the publicist and agent. We've got to get ahead of this." She noticed Mom's confused expression and added, "Damage control before the tabloids spin their own version of events. Please, not a word of this to anyone."

Would the tabloids be so ruthless that they would sensationalize a tragic death? That was the first thing that crossed my mind. The second thing was the Rocklin curse. What were the odds of tragedy striking the mansion's very first guests?

Abby was already on her phone making arrangements when the front door opened.

"Look who I found wandering around the house." The tall, muscular man standing in the hall doorway was the same man who had been present at the crew check-in at the inn. Beside him was Aunt Pearl, looking small and scrawny in comparison.

Her guilty expression made me immediately suspicious. She was fearful of the curse, yet she had returned to the mansion anyway. She was definitely up to something, but what exactly, was a mystery.

Mom sprung from her seat. "Pearl! You're supposed to be back at the inn."

"I came to get you two before it's too late." She shifted uneasily from one foot to the other.

Tyler turned and cast a quizzical look. "Too late for what?"

Nobody answered. Aunt Pearl focused on Mom, and I, in turn, focused on the man in the doorway. Now I remembered where I had seen him before. He had appeared in a few Real McCoys episodes in nonspeaking roles. His height and piercing green eyes made him hard to forget.

Serena cleared her throat. "This is Danny Nastasio, my driver. He was with Abby and me when we were out shopping earlier."

Danny acknowledged us with a nod. He walked over and stood at the edge of the sofa beside Serena.

"All three of you were all together the whole time?" Tyler asked.

Serena nodded. "Danny stayed in the car while we shopped, but he was parked right out front and he waited there the whole time. We were there a couple of hours, right Abby?"

Abby put her hand over her phone. "That's right. Bunny said that we were her only customers so far today, so I'm sure she'll remember us."

"I sure hope so. That woman is a bit forgetful and confused," Serena said. "She undercharged me by half, and then gave me back too much change. I only bought an outfit because I felt sorry for the poor woman. The clothes in there are ten years out of date. No wonder her business is losing money. She should probably sell the place and retire."

My dress was from Bunny's Key to Fashion. Granted, a lot of her inventory was long past its prime, but my dress was a classic style, a found treasure. Suddenly, I doubted myself. Was the gorgeous beaded dress that was too small to slide past my butt, out of style?

Pearl remained in the doorway. "Look what you've done, Ruby."

Mom's frozen lip trembled, and she looked ready to burst into tears.

"Who are you and why are you still here?" Serena demanded.

"This is Pearl West, my aunt. She came here because we're needed back at the Westwick Corners inn. If you don't mind, we'll head back." I hoped my lie gave us an excuse to leave Tyler to conduct a proper interview. I also wondered about Serena's crew back at the inn. Lucky was AWOL, Aunt Pearl was here with Mom and me. That left Grandma Vi all alone. Most importantly, it left our guests unfed and unattended to.

Tyler interjected, "Ruby, you go with Pearl and I'll drive Cen home later. Cen will take notes."

I looked to Serena for an objection. She gave an indifferent shrug.

I got my pen and notebook out and turned to a blank page. Hopefully I could use some of my notes for a story, but I'd have to clear that with Tyler first. Tabloid stories weren't my forte, but this was shaping up to be a blockbuster. Secret vows and sinister accidents in a secretive, small town made for suspenseful page-turners.

Serena almost certainly would find a way to work this into her show. Once she did, I would be free to report on it. I hadn't signed any nondisclosure agreements and didn't intend to. Things had just gotten a lot more interesting.

"What the hell is all this?' Jason McCoy stood in the living room entryway, the front door wide open behind him.

Serena dabbed her eyes with a tissue. "Jason, I have something to tell you. Sit down."

He eyed her suspiciously. "Why? Where's Dad?"

Serena turned to Tyler. "You tell him. I don't have the heart to."

CHAPTER 16

Once Tyler had relayed the bad news to Jason, he asked Jason to account for his whereabouts over the last few hours.

"I went to the Witching Post to get a drink. The bartender will remember me because I left him a very nice tip." Jason stood in front of the fireplace, shifting from one foot to the other.

"Where did you go after that?" Tyler asked.

"I came straight here. Are we done?" He glanced toward the hall as if planning his escape.

I remembered that Jason's Porsche wasn't parked outside the Witching Post when I had left the inn, and he wasn't exactly a slow driver. He was almost certainly lying.

"Can anyone confirm that?" Tyler asked.

Jason glanced at me before saying, "The bartender."

"Who was tending bar?"

Jason shrugged. "I don't know his name, but I'm sure

you're smart enough to figure it out. I'll be upstairs." He walked past us into the hall without another word.

After he left, Serena said, "Jason argued with Steve this morning. Ruby and Cendrine were here too and witnessed the whole thing. He left in a rage, angry because we refused to give him any more money. He's never worked for anything in his life. Steve paid for his expensive sports car, and we've been funding his drug habit too. We finally wrote him out of the show because of his addiction."

"Do you think Jason would harm Steve?" Tyler asked.

"What? No! Of course not." Serena sniffled. "Jason's an entitled rich kid. He acts out a lot and is always asking for money, but killing Steve? That's like killing the golden goose."

"Did Steve have any enemies that you know of? Anyone that wanted to harm him?" Tyler studied Serena closely.

"I-I don't think so. At least not enough to kill him," Serena said. "I thought you said it was an accident?"

Tyler shook his head. "I never said that. The preliminary conclusion on why he died is drowning, but how that happened exactly still needs to be confirmed by the medical examiner."

Abby interrupted. "Which means it's an accident."

"It's too early to say," Tyler said as his phone buzzed. He listened to the caller and grunted a few words in reply. He replaced the phone in his pocket, a troubled look on his face.

"Everything all right?" Abby asked.

Tyler stood and motioned for me to follow. "Don't go anywhere without checking with me first. I'll be in touch later this afternoon."

CHAPTER 17

Tyler had joined us for a late dinner at the inn. We ate in the kitchen, after a few busy hours of preparing and serving dinner to our guests in the dining room. By the time we ate and cleaned up, it was after 8 p.m. Mom and Aunt Pearl had already gone to the Witching Post to tend bar and serve drinks.

As we walked the short distance to the bar, we passed Jason's Porsche. It was backed into a spot near the driveway, ready for a quick getaway. There were other vehicles there too, including Serena's white Mercedes.

We entered the bar and found it packed full of a half-drunk crew. Serena and company were also present. Thankfully, they had heeded Tyler's request not to leave town.

Abby stood on the stage that was normally used for live music and debriefed everyone about Steve's tragic death. There wasn't much to tell, at least not officially.

I had been waiting anxiously for Tyler to fill me on the

ME's latest update. We sat at a small table set in a quiet corner of the bar, distanced from the other tables. No one could eavesdrop on our conversation, and from our vantage point, we could see anyone approaching.

"This is much better," Tyler said. "It's noisy enough that no one will overhear our conversation."

Mom, behind the bar helping Aunt Pearl, spotted us and smiled.

Tyler motioned her over and then turned back to me. "The ME told me that she found no water in Steve's lungs, indicating that he didn't drown. Drowning victims have water in their lungs. They die by asphyxia, as the air in their lungs is replaced by water. They suffocate because they can't breathe."

I gasped. "Steve was already dead when he entered the water?"

Tyler nodded. "Steve died from blunt force trauma. He was either hit on the head or else he fell and hit his head. But I don't think he fell on the pool deck. The size and location of his wound makes that unlikely. The ME believes that he was hit on the side of the head with a large blunt object, possibly a weapon of some sort."

"She thinks it's murder?" I whispered.

"She didn't go that far. She's ruled it an undetermined cause of death due to blunt force trauma to the head. That's as far as she will go, because no murder weapon was found and there weren't any obvious signs of a struggle either. She can't for sure say whether it's a homicide unless more evidence points that way. Her choices were accidental, homicide, natural causes, such as a heart attack or stroke, suicide, or undetermined."

"That's it, then? No more investigation?" I sipped my Diet Coke as my stomach growled.

"I didn't say that. I still have to check out everyone's alibis and possible motives. But the narrow time window eliminates almost everybody, if Ruby saw Steve just a few minutes before he died."

Mom stood beside me and had been quietly listening. She pulled out a chair and sat down. "You think Steve was killed?"

"It's just one of many possibilities, but we can't rule it out," Tyler said.

Mom drew in a deep breath. "I guess I didn't make this clear before, but uh…I didn't actually see Steve. I only heard him. I knocked a few times before he told me to come in and leave the flower arrangement samples on the kitchen counter, which I did. Just as I was leaving, I remembered that I had some questions about the menu that couldn't wait. It seemed silly to shout back and forth, so I just went out to the pool because I knew he was swimming. I don't understand how he could be alive one moment and dead the next."

"Are you positive it was Steve you were speaking to?" I asked. "Did you recognize his voice?"

"I thought it was him, yes. I may have only met him once in real life, but I've been watching that show for years. I'm positive it was his voice. On the other hand, I wasn't expecting anyone else to be impersonating him, so I didn't think twice about it." Mom's eyes widened. "You think someone else was there?"

Tyler placed his hand on Ruby's. "I don't know yet but I'm going to find out."

Mom turned to me. "Cen, not a word of this to Pearl. She'll do something drastic if it turns out that the voice I heard wasn't actually Steve. She'll blame the curse."

"Not a word from you to anyone, Ruby," Tyler said.

I nodded. "Could it have been Jason speaking to you, Mom? His car was already gone from the Witching Post parking lot when you called. He sounds a bit like Steve. He could have lied about where he was. Was his car still parked at the Witching Post when you left?"

Mom frowned. "I think it was already gone when I left too. I don't remember seeing it, but I was so focused on getting the flower samples over to the McCoys that I wasn't really paying much attention."

"Who else had access to the house?" I asked. "The more people we can eliminate, the easier it is to narrow it down. Danny, Serena's driver probably also had access to the house."

Mom shook her head. "I gave them two sets of keys, but Danny drove Serena and Abby shopping, remember? They probably took a key. They were at Bunny's Key to Fashion. Did you talk to Bunny yet?"

Tyler nodded. "She confirmed everything. I wish I had something more than an eyewitness account though. They're often unreliable, and I don't want to rule anyone out at this point."

"Am I a suspect?" Mom's eyes widened.

"In theory, yes. However, Steve was at least seven or eight inches taller than you. Unless you were standing on a ladder or a step or something, you're not tall enough to hit him on the head. It was a forceful blow too, by a fairly strong person."

"You think I'm short and weak?"

It was hard to tell whether Mom was serious or just giving Tyler a hard time.

Tyler apparently couldn't tell either. "Of course not, Ruby. You're one of the strongest people I know. I haven't completely ruled out anyone yet, including you. But given the evidence so far, I'm looking in another direction."

"Speaking of other directions, I'd better go back to the inn and check whether Pearl cleaned all the rooms while our guests are still here at the bar." Mom slid back her chair and wearily rose to her feet. "It's been a long day."

Once Mom was out of earshot, Tyler leaned closer. "Let's talk motives. The spouse is the killer at least eighty percent of the time. I discovered that Steve and Serena took out big life insurance policies on each other a few months ago. A fatal slip and fall resulting in accidental death doubles the payout."

I was doubtful. "They're filthy rich from their reality show, so they don't need the money. And without Steve, there is no more Real McCoys show. It doesn't make financial sense. On top of that, they seemed to be so much in love."

"You've got to be kidding, Cen. They're constantly bickering on every episode."

"You've seen the show?"

"Everybody's seen that show. I wish I could un-see it. It's over the top ridiculous."

"It's just life exaggerated. The shock value is what makes it popular with everybody. They're really quite sweet and down to earth in real life," I said.

Tyler laughed. "You're so impressed at their celebrity

status that you aren't looking at things objectively. I would never treat you the way they treat each other on screen, even if it is all an act."

"It's just for the ratings." I sighed. "It makes—or would have made—their vow renewal ceremony all the more romantic."

"You think that's romantic? Just wait till tomorrow night." Tyler reached across the table and grabbed my hand. "I'm going to surprise you."

"I can't wait." In truth, I was afraid. Very afraid that Aunt Pearl wouldn't locate the engagement ring in time to replace it in Tyler's pocket. Diamond rings were expensive, but our relationship was priceless, and I couldn't bear to damage it.

CHAPTER 18

I waited at the bar while Aunt Pearl refilled our drinks. "Any luck on finding the ring, Aunt Pearl?"

"You get rid of these people and maybe I'll have some time to look." She slammed the two glasses down on the bar so hard that they spilled.

"You better find it. And you better not interfere in the investigation."

Aunt Pearl scrubbed an imaginary spot on the bar. "Don't threaten me, Cendrine. I'll do what I can when I'm good and ready. Ruby's greed brought all this on. Talk to her. Maybe it's not too late to reverse the curse."

I had no good answer, so I took the two glasses and carried them back to our table. "I keep coming back to Jason," I said to Tyler. I explained the time discrepancy between Jason's timeline and his missing car when I left the inn for the Rocklin mansion.

Tyler nodded. "Jason has multiple motives, but why would he leave Serena, his stepmom, alive? He would have presumably inherited everything if they both died. Instead, she gets it all."

"That's true if it was premeditated," I said. "Maybe he killed his dad in a fit of rage."

We spent the next hour-and-a-half painstakingly going over the details. Serena and Abby's claim of shopping together at the time of Steve's death had checked out, giving them each an alibi. Serena and Abby had shopped at Bunny's Key to Fashion, while Danny waited outside the store in plain view of the two women as well as Bunny, the store owner, who had vouched for all three of them.

"They all alibi each other, but do you believe their story?" I asked.

Tyler shrugged. "It doesn't matter what I believe if the alibi checks out. Bunny confirmed everything, but I still need to check the cameras." Luckily Bunny's store was on Main Street, and some of the shops had security cameras. The footage would either corroborate or contradict their statements. It was just a matter of time to review the camera footage.

"Bunny's confirmation isn't all that reliable since her memory isn't that great anymore." Bunny was in the early stages of dementia. She still operated the store she loved, but with limited hours and lots of help. Trusted friends dropped by for coffee and a chat, but she made very few actual sales. Bunny could afford to close the store and retire, but it stayed open because Bunny loved it. It gave her purpose.

"That's true," Tyler said. "I called Gertie to confirm but she's away on a Caribbean cruise. No one else was able to cover her shift, so Bunny was working alone in the store." Gertie normally helped Bunny during the week. She would be flabbergasted when she returned from her cruise and discovered all that she had missed.

Tyler said, "The ME places Steve's time of death within an hour of Ruby's discovery. That was based on his undigested stomach contents. Of course, we already knew that, but it does validate Ruby's accounting of events. It's such a short timeframe that it's hard to fathom someone committing the murder and leaving no trace. You and Ruby saw Steve with Serena at around 10 am. Shortly after Serena, Abby and Danny left for shopping, Ruby returns and talks to someone who sounded exactly like Steve around 11:30. Moments later, Ruby discovers Steve dead in the pool."

"That's a very small time-window for an equally small number of people with both the means and opportunity to kill him," I agreed.

Tyler nodded. "This should be easy to figure out."

"There could be another explanation. Maybe someone followed them here?"

"Like a stalker?" Tyler asked.

"Possibly. But it does seem more personal than random. Assuming that it really is murder, and not just a tragic accident."

Tyler nodded. "Let's look at this another way. We need to rule out accidental death. Ruby did a great job of updating, but the Rocklin place is old and full of hazards. Some of the paving stones are uneven, and the patio is very slippery walking in bare feet because it's covered in frost. The cold would be painful even. Why would anyone walk barefoot across an icy cement patio in freezing temperatures?"

"Steve was wearing flip-flops on his feet when we saw him earlier. I'm sure of it. Did he forget his flip-flops when he went outside?"

Tyler shook his head. "Ruby didn't see his flip-flops by the pool, and the Shady Creek police couldn't find any inside or outside the house."

"The distance from the door to the pool edge is at least twenty feet," I said. "Steve had to walk to get to the pool. Shoes or no shoes, he left no footprints. The patio was covered in frost, so why weren't there imprints left by his footsteps as he walked to the pool?" I flashed back to my bum print from my earlier fall. My butt had certainly made an impression, so why hadn't Steve's footprints? Steve, a man easily twice my size, couldn't have possibly walked on the frosty surface without leaving a mark.

Tyler scratched his chin thoughtfully. "You're right about that. No footprints all the way from the patio door to the pool. Nothing else either. No wheel tracks if he was moved there. He's a big man, so I doubt that one single person could carry him without help. It's been below freezing all day, so the ice couldn't have melted and refroze again."

"Can you even have an accident with absolutely nothing disturbed around the pool? No sign of a slip and fall? I don't think so. Doesn't the absence of things that should be there indicate foul play of some sort?"

We sat in silence for a few minutes, surrounded by the growing din of voices, some of the patrons getting drunk.

"Good point, Cen," Tyler said. "Let's say for now that it is murder. Serena insisted that no one other than cast and crew even knew the McCoys were in town, but someone local could have been curious enough to snoop around. Maybe they saw signs of activity at the mansion and they trespassed onto the property. They got surprised by Steve, and then things turned ugly."

I was skeptical. "Most people think the Rocklin mansion is haunted and are afraid to even walk past it, let alone trespass on the property. If they were curious, the security gate and fencing would have stopped them. I don't see any signs of forced entry."

Tyler sighed. "An intruder could have climbed over the fence, even over those tall spikes. The intrusion would have been caught on the security cameras, of course, which I'm hoping are all operational. The cameras cover most of the property, but there are a few blind spots. I'm in the process of getting the footage checked out."

"My hunch says it's personal," I said. "The killer knew Steve was at the mansion, and also had access." People killed for personal gain. Hired assassins did it for the money, but since they were hired by someone, it circled back to being personal in some way. Friends, family, and business associates often had multiple motives. Money and power, ego, secrets, jealousy, and fear drove otherwise normal people to commit the most heinous crimes. There were probably a few people with a target on Steve McCoy's back.

Tyler nodded. "Hardly anyone had access to the mansion, and therefore the opportunity to kill Steve. "Serena, Jason, Abby, Danny the chauffeur. And your Mom."

"Mom wouldn't kill one of her customers."

He held up his hand in protest. "I know she's not a killer, and she's not physically able to kill someone twice her size. On the other hand, she was the last person to see him alive. I also have a close personal relationship with your Mom, and I need to be objective. I need some evidence to definitely rule her out."

Tyler was right. He was, I hoped, Mom's future son-in-law. I prayed that the engagement ring had somehow made it back into Tyler's jacket pocket. He was wearing a different jacket now and had been earlier too. Maybe he hadn't yet noticed the ring missing from his jacket in the Jeep's backseat.

"I still think Jason's hiding something. He fought with Steve and Serena about money, and he was recently fired from the show. He's still financially dependent on Steve and Serena. He's got a drug problem, making him desperate and willing to go to great lengths to get money. They could have physically fought, and Steve slipped and had a fatal fall. Afterward, Jason altered his timeline to give himself an alibi, and he cleaned up everything around the pool. It could explain the missing footwear." I mentioned the conversation between Jason and Lucky. "I didn't hear any specifics other than the mention of money, but it sounded very suspicious."

It was as if Tyler hadn't heard a word. "There's no evidence either way. No blood and no murder weapon. The ME thinks it's within the realm of possibly that he was hit with a blunt object first, and knocked unconscious, but says she can't state that he was hit unless there is concrete evidence proving that. I need her to change the cause of death from undetermined, Cen. Otherwise the district attorney will never charge."

"Maybe the forensics team didn't look hard enough for a murder weapon," I said. "Wouldn't any half-decent killer take the murder weapon with them? Whoever did it was smart enough to literally cover their tracks in the frost."

"The ME won't rule it a homicide without more proof. At a minimum that means definitive evidence of what caused the wound that killed Steve. She's under pressure to complete her report. She will probably call the cause of death undetermined. Without a murder weapon—"

"The killer goes free," I said.

"It's such a high-profile case, Cen. She's double-checking everything right now, but even though it looks like someone came along after Steve's death and did some sort of a clean-up, that's not enough. Without concrete evidence showing something sinister, it's going to get ruled undetermined."

"Someone hit Steve in the head, Tyler. I know it, you know it, and the ME knows it. So why can't she just say so?"

He hesitated. "Undetermined still leaves things open for if and when new evidence turns up. But each hour and day that we don't find something works against that happening. If we don't find something now, chances of finding it weeks, months, or years from now are slim. Serena's lawyer is already pressuring Brayden. She's threatening to sue Westwick Corners if this drags out and becomes a scandal."

Brayden Banks, our town's mayor and my former fiancée, had zero backbone. Pressure on him meant he would apply the pressure on Tyler too. Brayden always avoided negative publicity or anything that could hinder his political aspirations. But this was a moral issue, not a financial one, and it was just plain wrong to let wealth and power influence an investigation.

I glanced over at Serena sitting at a large table with her entourage, reminiscing about her late husband. She seemed genuinely sad. Was it real, or was it all an act like The Real McCoys?

I picked up the conversation. "Why is Brayden even involved? It's a police investigation looking for a medical cause of death. It's not political and Serena can't sue the town." She could certainly sue Mom for an accident on the premises though. I feared that would come next. If it did, we would be financially ruined. A sense of dread enveloped me.

"It's probably just a scare tactic, but Serena won't back down," Tyler said. "She wants a quick resolution so the story goes away. She said that all the negative publicity decreases her future earning potential."

"Steve was one-half of the Real McCoys. Serena loses money no matter what. It's not the town's fault."

Tyler sighed. "I know. Trouble is, even a frivolous lawsuit could bankrupt the town with legal fees. We'd have to defend ourselves in court and that costs money. Unless we find concrete evidence, we can't hold things up without a good reason. We simply don't have deep enough pockets to fight a millionaire celebrity, Cen."

"One thing I know for sure is that If my husband suddenly died, I wouldn't rush the investigation. I would want every investigative angle pursued."

Tyler's face reddened. "That's uh…really good to know."

That subject we had been avoiding suddenly thrust itself into the forefront. My pulse quickened as I tried to explain myself. "I just meant that, um…Serena changed from wanting to renew her vows to a decision to bury her husband awfully quick. She should want to take the time for a proper investigation, especially if the ME can't provide definitive answers."

"You would think she would, but not everyone thinks like that. Especially when the evidence isn't black and white."

I frowned. "Suing the town is what a bully does, not a grieving spouse. Besides, Steve died on private property. How is that the town's responsibility?"

"The lawyers will claim that the town never inspected the swimming pool. If they had, it would have been obvious that the pool was not built to code."

"Do we even have a building code? We're barely a village. How is that even connected to Steve's death?"

He said, "It's not. But just the claim will land us in court, and we can't afford a lawsuit." Tyler lowered his voice. "Cen, I need to ask you something important."

Our brainstorming had changed the focus from accidental to murder, but had it also changed the timing of my wedding proposal? What if Aunt Pearl hadn't located the missing ring?

"Cen? You listening?" Tyler's voice broke into my thoughts.

"Uh, yes," I gulped. Years from now, we would both look back nostalgically at this moment, as strange as it was. It wasn't the least bit romantic, but love was what mattered. Maybe it wasn't a fancy dinner, but I was too fat to zip up my new red dress anyway. I took a deep breath and leaned closer to Tyler. "Ask away."

He leaned in closer and placed his hand over mine.

"What I need to know is, is there any magic involved?"

"*That's* your question?" That was *not* the question I had expected. As I exhaled and slumped down in my chair, my newly acquired belly fat squeezed together and pushed up against my underwire bra. How depressing. On the plus side, a romantic proposal was surely coming my way very soon. Wasn't it? Or was I completely wrong about everything?

"Why are you upset?" Tyler asked.

"I-I'm not upset." I bit my lower lip and avoided Tyler's gaze.

"Yes, you are. You always squint when you're mad. Something's bothering you and I don't know what it is."

I should have told Tyler right then that, yes, magic was involved. But was I even allowed to tell him about the Rocklin curse? Somehow, I didn't think so. Did talking about the curse bring on more curse? Either way, it would infuriate Aunt Pearl, which wasn't worth the trouble. What would she do to me? Curse me?

And I certainly couldn't mention a ring that I wasn't supposed to know about.

Apparently, I was already cursed, with my pound-an-hour weight gain and Mom's get-rich-quick scheme amounting to a dead body and a whole lot of bad publicity.

I was mad. Irrationally mad, but so what. Everything was going wrong and I needed to be mad at someone besides myself. Witchcraft or no witchcraft, our family would remain divided in a blame game, and once again it was up to me to find a solution. I had to somehow make this curse go away.

But I couldn't take it out on Tyler. So instead, I said, "I just hate the idea of someone getting away with murder."

"Then prove that it is murder, Cen. Help me find the murder weapon."

CHAPTER 19

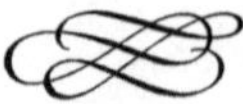

It was a mix of rain and snow by the time I left The Witching Post. Tyler had departed a few minutes earlier. He drove back to his office to review surveillance footage. I was headed to the Rocklin Mansion. Creepy yes, but with Serena and gang settled in at the bar, it would probably be my only chance to have another look around the pool. But my real goal was to banish the curse, once and for all.

To recap, I now had three almost-impossible goals:

1. Find the murder weapon,
2. Solve the murder and set the story straight to shut down Serena's claims of accidental death
3. Banish the curse

Those goals brought further goals. If I could solve the murder, I would have a scoop on the story of Steve's tragic death before anyone else. In short, I had a lot riding on this. The freezing rain soaked through my jacket as I ran to my SUV at the other end of the parking lot. I jumped into the driver's seat and mentally reviewed my to-do list before starting the car.

Finding the murder weapon—if there was one—should be pretty straightforward, witchcraft-wise. In theory, all I had to do was return to the Rocklin mansion and do a rewind spell to replay the events, one by one. Obviously, I couldn't tell Tyler my plans. So here I was, scared and hopeful on the road to the Rocklin mansion. Or, quite possibly, the road to ruin.

Reversing the chain of events required rewind spell on top of rewind spell, on top of rewind spell. Mistakes could literally spell disaster, because if anything went wrong in any of the reversals, I could potentially alter history for every single person who had attended the Rocklin Mansion today. That included the McCoys, their employees, as well as the police and firefighters. It even included Tyler and me, as well as my family. It was an unsurmountable amount of multitasking for interdependent events, even for me. So many people had been on scene, and so many hours had passed.

But maybe there was another way. I doubted the crime scene techs had missed an obvious murder weapon, but what if it was unlike any murder weapon they had expected to find?

I had an inkling of an idea, but I needed help from another witch. Mom was out of the question. She was still traumatized over all that had happened, and yet somehow had to carry on and make dinner for our guests. Besides, since Mom had discovered Steve's body, she was directly involved. Aunt Pearl was also a no-no, even if she wasn't already occupied tending bar.

There was only one witch who I could lean on, and that was Grandma Vi.

* * *

THE DRIVE to the Rocklin mansion was treacherous. The sleet had turned to hail soon after I left the Witching Post. Icy pellets pummeled the windshield and ricocheted off the hood. I squinted at the road ahead. In the dark, the road was barely visible, with the hail falling too fast for the windshield wipers to keep up.

Grandma Vi floated a few inches above the front passenger seat, admonishing me for what I was about to do. "You lied to Tyler by telling him you were staying home, and you tricked me into leaving the house! I'm not setting foot on Rocklin soil. Turn this car around and get out of this cursed place. Take me back home, right now!"

"I can't until I find what I'm looking for." I kept my voice casual as I drove through the Rocklin gates. "Just a momentary detour. I think I can get rid of the curse, but it has to be done here. The curse only exists because we think it does."

I only half-believed that myself, but that was just one of the reasons for my visit.

As I reached the parking lot, I pressed the brake when I spotted Serena's white Mercedes SUV. It had been parked at the Witching Post when I left, and I hadn't seen her leave. She must have left the bar after I had, but got on the road sooner, while I sat parked in the lot. No cars had passed me on the only road here.

Suddenly loud voices drifted outside. I took my foot off the brake pedal, ready to switch to the gas pedal for a quick getaway but stopped. I wasn't sure about my plan anymore, especially when I recognized the laughter. But this was my only chance. I had to carry out my plan now or it would never happen. And I had to do so without getting discovered.

Serena was drunk. Her words were slurred, and what she said next shocked me.

"Jason's responsible for this. If he had been home, this never would have happened. Steve wouldn't have been swimming alone." Serena hiccupped. "Or maybe it wouldn't have mattered. Jason probably would have let Steve die."

"You don't mean that." Abby's voice was equally distinctive, even at a distance. But unlike Serena, she was sober.

"Yes, I do. Jason will be glad that Steve's dead. No love lost between those two. He probably wishes I was dead too."

As much as I wanted to stay right there within earshot, anyone looking out the window would have noticed me. I drove slowly and parked at the far end of the driveway, furthest from the backyard and pool. My vehicle was still visible, but only if someone leaving the house turned and looked backward. I exited the SUV and crept toward the voices to listen. Grandma Vi floated a few feet behind me. One of the large living room French doors was wide open. It faced the front of the house and was surrounded by a small porch with a sitting area, bordered by a two-foot-high brick wall. Even in the darkness, anyone looking outside would easily discover us if they bothered to look. I crouched in the grass near the wall, deciding it was worth the risk. I hoped to glean some information from their conversation. I was soon disappointed when the talk turned to food.

"I'm hungry," Serena complained. "There's nothing to eat in this town."

"I'll call Ruby and ask her to bring something over," Abby said.

"If her cooking is anything like her baking, I'd rather starve."

Grandma Vi gasped. "The nerve of that woman!"

"Quiet!" I waved my hand and immediately regretted it, since no one could hear Grandma Vi but me. They could certainly hear me though.

"What was that noise?" Abby asked.

"What noise? Let's head to Shady Creek and find a decent restaurant. I'm craving Italian." Serena burst into tears. "Pasta was Steve's favorite meal."

"Grab your things and I'll get the car," a male voice said.

I guessed it was Danny, Serena's driver.

I would be discovered unless I moved. My heart thumped as I knelt down and crawled past the patio and the open doors, the short wall hiding me from view. Once past it, I stood and crept past the front entrance and around to the opposite side of the house where the pool was. Aside from the second set of French doors leading to the pool, this part of the house was windowless. Thankfully those doors were closed with the blinds drawn. I positioned myself near the side entrance and the laurel hedge, where I was unlikely to be spotted. It was out of sight, both from inside the house and from the front where Serena's SUV was parked. We only had to wait for them to leave.

There was one problem. My car was parked outside. Maybe they would be in a hurry to leave and wouldn't look to the side of the house to see it. I held my breath and hoped for the best, all the while preparing myself for the worst.

I drew in a deep breath as I pondered my next steps.

Grandma Vi flitted back and forth, distraught. "You cannot set foot in that house, Cendrine."

"I don't need to go in." Admitting I had already been inside would only upset her more. Grandma Vi hovered beside me as I pressed my body flush against the tall laurel hedge. The sharp branches painfully poked against my winter jacket and jeans, creating painful pressure points all over my arms and legs as I pressed my body further into the foliage.

Then the front door slammed, quickly followed by footsteps and voices that receded with each passing second. Moments later, car doors slammed and an engine started. Car tires crunched gravel and finally there was silence. I peeked around the hedge just in time to see taillights disappear down around the bend in the driveway. This was my only chance to see what I could unearth with a spell. The odds were slim that my plan could work, but it was worth a shot.

Grandma floated fifteen feet above me as a lookout. Her vantage point allowed her to alert me if anyone came up the Rocklin Mansion driveway or if any more people emerged from the house. I doubted anyone was still inside, but I couldn't know for sure.

She whispered, "Hurry up, Cendrine! Every minute we spend here is a minute too long."

My pulse quickened as I stood on the concrete patio beside the pool with my flashlight, scanning the area for anything that didn't belong. Like a murder weapon. It was ridiculous to think I'd find anything since the police had already scoured the area. They probably hadn't missed anything, but it was worth a second look, even if it was in the dark. It was a last-ditch attempt to prove my theory that Steve's death was anything but an accident. It wasn't the main reason I was here though.

Grandma read my mind. "Anything is possible, but

you've got to actually *do* something, right now. Stop standing around and do it."

"Okay, okay, but rushing stresses me out." Truth was, I was nervous. Nervous that I wouldn't be able to pull off the spell on a property where our witch powers had been dramatically diminished. Mom's powers hadn't worked at all when she tried to save Steve. Why would mine work now?

No.

Think positive.

I took a deep breath in and stepped closer to the pool. I focused my thoughts. Holding my hands up, palms outward, I said:

SOMETHING HERE DOES NOT BELONG,
Make it visible before too long,

REVEAL *the weapon that caused the blow,*
Help us find and catch the foe.

I WAITED, but nothing happened.

"Try turning in a different direction," Grandma Vi suggested.

I turned to my left and repeated the spell.

Still nothing.

I turned once again and recited the spell. No matter which direction I turned, nothing happened.

I gazed up at Grandma Vi. "Am I doing something wrong?"

She frowned. "No, it's this cursed place. Our spells don't seem to work here. Or it could be that it was just an accident and there's no weapon to find. We may never know."

"There must be something else I can try. A different spell maybe?" I could leave now, but then this risky operation would have been all for nothing.

Grandma Vi sighed. "Nothing will work, unless you break the one and only spell that's stopping everything else. The Rocklin Curse."

I panned my flashlight around the pool area one last time. No murder weapons of any kind, not so much as a pool noodle. I turned to walk back to the gate.

At that moment my flashlight shone on something. A flash of white underneath the hedge caught my eye. "Wait! Maybe my spell worked after all. I found something."

I walked closer and knelt down. I stretched my arm underneath the hedge. My hand closed on a small piece of paper, soggy, wet, and covered with dirt. I carefully lifted it and wiped it with my fingers to reveal numbers in light purple-blue ink.

"What is it?" Grandma asked.

I stood and placed the paper under the light. "It's not a murder weapon, unfortunately. Just an old-fashioned cash register receipt." There were no details identifying the items purchased, just 3 lines with prices, identified as item 1, item 2, item 3.

I was about to throw it away when Grandma Vi descended to take a closer look.

She peered over my shoulder. "Hmmm. Things aren't

always obvious, Cen. It could be a clue that leads you to the weapon."

"You're just trying to make me feel better." I had imagined the murder weapon to be something heavy like a brick or a rock, not a simple piece of paper. But Grandma could be right. My mind flashed to a game I used to play as a kid.

Rock, paper, scissors.

The rules of the game were that rock crushes scissors, scissors cut paper, and paper covers rock. *Paper covers rock.* It could be a sign, but of what? I had no idea. Spells often turned out to be different than expected for many reasons. Was the receipt some sort of sick Rocklin curse joke? I doubted that the Shady Creek police would have missed such obvious evidence during their investigation. Yet I wasn't totally convinced the receipt had materialized as a result of my spell.

Magical or nonmagical, I knew of a local place that issued receipts exactly like that. At the very least, I should check it out. If I hurried, I could make it there before it closed for lunch. But first, there was one last thing I had to do.

Grandma Vi floated near the gate, clearly rattled. "We need to leave, now! I'm feeling weak with the pull of this place. It's bad, Cen."

"I know, I feel it too. I-I just need enough time to be sure I say the words right." I stood at the pool beside the exact spot where Steve's body had floated hours earlier. It was now or never, but I didn't want to rush the spell and screw it up, particularly with a spell that could undo a decades-long curse.

"Every moment we linger lessens our witch powers. It's very dangerous for us to be here. Just recite the darn spell." She dropped a paper from her translucent pocket.

I grabbed the paper as it wafted downward. I unfolded it to see a typed version of the same spell that Aunt Pearl had recited earlier at the inn with no success. My plan of reciting the spell directly on the Rocklin property was a long shot. I was thankful for the written version instead of reciting from memory.

I took a deep breath and hoped for a miracle:

I BLAST your curse from the skies,
I extinguish it before your eyes,
You shall not burden us again,
Go away with all your ken,
I will guard and protect this place,
Do not dare to show your face,
Your witchy powers are no more,
Forever locked behind the door,
Forever changed from witch to mortal,
Eternally banished from the portal,
You will pay for your grave misdeeds,
All your dreams will die as seeds,
No more will your curses sprout,
For eternity, you shall live in doubt,
Forevermore and a day,
Which time you shall stay away.

GRANDMA VI GASPED. "Cen, you said it wrong! It's forty years and a day, not forevermore and a d—"

I pointed at the paper and shook my head. "No, it says forevermore right here."

"Why then, did Pearl say forty years? She wouldn't make a dumb mistake like that."

I reread the paper. "It definitely says forever. Forever is what we want, right?"

Grandma Vi squinted at the paper. "Oh, my, you're right! I remember now...there are different versions of the spell. The timeframe changed when a WICCA rule got revised many years ago. One word changed everything."

Her voice was drowned out by a rumbling sky. Everything turned dark as the thunder increased, followed a minute later with a downpour of rain.

Rain?

Odd, since the temperature was below freezing. It was far too cold for anything but snow.

Yet it was rain. Warm, sloppy raindrops soaked me like a tropical downpour, not the frigid, bone-chilling rain that usually fell in Washington state.

Grandma Vi's transparent form floated toward me, unaffected by the sudden downpour. She clapped her hands together. "I feel stronger already. You did it, Cen! You broke the curse!"

Nothing had changed that I could see, but I felt a lightness, almost a giddiness as I turned my face skyward. I laughed as warm raindrops fell on my upturned face. I felt peace in my soul. Something in the air soothed me and energized me at the same time.

An invisible weight I hadn't felt before was suddenly lifted off my back. Everything felt lighter, like gravity had shifted. Even my waistband was looser. "One little word and everything changes? How is that?"

"WICCA outlawed 'forever' spells years ago, when they implemented time limits on spells."

"If that's the case, then why did my spell work and not Aunt Pearl's? I said forevermore and a day. Aunt Pearl said forty years and a day. Her spell should have worked, not mine."

"You would think so," Grandma Vi said. "But a mistake was made. The original Rocklin curse was forevermore, but when the WICCA rule commuted the maximum sentences to forty years, the original curse was recast with forty years. The counter spell was forty years too."

"If that's the case, then the curse should have expired years ago when the forty years was up," I said.

"There was an appeal on the forty-year time limit and after a few years, WICCA changed their minds. They applied the forty-year time limit only to new spells, not pre-existing ones. The original 'forever' curse on pre-existing spells was re-instated. There are very few forever spells left. I guess Pearl updated her spell book for the original change to forty years but didn't record the change back to forever."

"How could our entire family miss this?"

"It's quite simple, Cen. The curse wasn't activated, so we felt no ill-effects. We thought that WICCA sorted out all the paperwork related to their rule change. We figured that the curse was completely canceled out by our original counter-spell. Except in this case, the original curse and the counter spell were still mismatched."

I was slowly catching on. "They couldn't cancel each other out because they were mismatched. The original Rocklin forevermore curse was reinstated, but because of WICCA's bureaucratic mistake, the forevermore counter-spell needed to be done a second time?"

Grandma Vi nodded. "Exactly. We really should have double-checked, but we trusted WICCA. You don't mess around with big curses like that. Casting one too many counter spells on powerful curses can have serious consequences."

"I'm free of a curse that I never knew existed. My life should improve dramatically then, right?" This could change everything. I could quite possibly eat anything and not gain an ounce. My newspaper would turn a profit with less effort. So would the inn and even Pearl's Charm School. Westwick Corners could flourish instead of existing as an almost-ghost town.

Grandma Vi intruded into my thoughts. "I doubt your life will change all that much. It can be hard to tell a curse from simple bad luck. The only sure sign is when the bad luck is something so far out of the ordinary. Then it's probably a curse."

"Like the hole in the ceiling, and the radio on fire?"

"The ceiling, yes. But the radio on fire really was me," Grandma Vi beamed. "I've still got what it takes."

"Aunt Pearl should have updated every spell in her spell book. At the very least, she should have remembered to do it."

Grandma Vi shook her head. "You know your aunt is terrible with details, and we're all getting older and more forgetful. I think that in the heat of the moment, when our ceiling opened up, she panicked."

"But Aunt Pearl's not afraid of anything or anyone," I said.

"She's afraid of a lot of things, Cen. She just hides it well. I should have listened to her spell better myself, but I was still flustered and distracted after messing up your computer. I'm so sorry I didn't notice the wording until now. I could have prevented a tragedy." Her aura pulsated between dark and light.

If ghosts could cry, Grandma Vi would be bawling. I touched her transparent shoulder. "It's nobody's fault, Grandma."

Her aura darkened. "It is my fault. The downfall of this town and everything else resulted from a curse we could have lifted decades ago. Imagine how different things could have been."

Except that if everything had turned out differently, then we would have led different lives. We would never have turned our home into an inn. Tyler never would have come to town to accept the sheriff job that nobody else wanted, and I would be married to someone else right now.

"I like everything as it is and I wouldn't change a thing, Grandma. As for Steve, there's a good chance his death has nothing to do with the curse."

Grandma Vi wiped an imaginary tear from her eye. "You really think so?"

I studied the receipt. "Our luck has changed in many ways."

CHAPTER 22

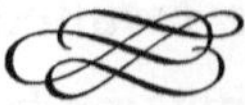

I pulled into the Gas N'Go and parked at the side of the building. Grandma Vi waited in the car. I walked past the empty gas island and up the single step to the store. As I pulled open the door and walked inside, I remembered Wilt, the former Gas N'Go cashier, who now languished in a Las Vegas jail. Cherise, his replacement, was the polar opposite of Wilt. She was helpful and friendly, and everyone in town loved her. In fact, she was almost too customer-focused and cheerful. She'd help a gun-toting robber fill his tank with a smile.

"Hey, Cen, haven't seen you in a while." Cherise stood behind the counter. "What can I get ya? The usual?"

My stomach growled as I eyed the tray of chocolate croissants in the glass display case. "No thanks. I'm here for something else."

Cherise pulled out a heart-shaped plate full of chocolates

from behind the counter. "Try a sample? We just got these in this morning."

I was tempted but wasn't about to risk my newly svelte waistline. The Gas N'Go sold the same chocolate assortment every year. I knew for a fact that they were mostly leftovers from last year's Valentine's Day. Or maybe even the Valentine's Day before that. We all did what we had to do in order make ends meet in a town with no jobs, and it wasn't always pretty.

I shook my head with feigned casualness instead of the desperation I felt inside. "No. I'm here for another reason."

"You sure? The chocolates are going fast. Maybe grab a box as a Valentine's gift for Tyler?" Cherise's right eye shut in an exaggerated wink. It would have been comical if she wasn't so obviously desperate.

I wanted my valentine surprise for Tyler to be unique, not the stale gas station chocolates Cherise was pushing. Time was running out though, and I had yet to come up with anything suitable. The downside of a small town was that everyone knew everybody else's business. Almost everybody, because I still couldn't figure out who had paid me for the full-page Valentine's Day ad.

"Uh…thanks Cherise. Maybe later."

"You hardly have any time left," Cherise's voice had a hint of desperation now. "It's almost Valentine's Day."

I had more important matters to deal with at the moment. "Actually, I'm here to ask a favor. You've got security cameras here, right?"

Cherise nodded and her smile vanished. She pointed to three monitors above the cash register. "One over the door, one above the gas pump, and one that covers the cash register. Why? Is something wrong?"

I couldn't breathe a word about the celebrities in our midst, let alone that one was now dead. The news would spread through town in an instant. "Nothing's wrong, exactly. It's just that Aunt Pearl did something crazy again. I need solid proof before I accuse her of anything. I also want to make things right for the store."

Cherise's eyes widened. "Pearl did something here, at the Gas N'Go? She's not up to her old pyromaniac tricks again, is she? I hope we don't have to go into lockdown again."

"No, no…nothing like that. There's just a slight chance of…of—" I held my hand up. "I can't accuse her without proof. It's probably nothing, but I need to check for safety's sake."

Aunt Pearl had once tried to blow up the gas station, so Cherise didn't question my odd request. Cherise was quite a busy body, but she was afraid of getting involved in any of Aunt Pearl's criminal pursuits.

"Yes, of course, Cen. Thanks for keeping us all safe." Cherise put the plate of chocolates down and came out from behind the counter. "What do you need?"

"Can I review your camera footage from the last day or two?"

Cherise shrugged. "I'm not really supposed to show it to people, but given the circumstances, I don't see what harm it would do. Just don't tell anyone."

I clasped my hands together. "I won't, I promise."

Cherise walked past me to the front door. "Give me a minute and I'll get you set up. I guess whatever Pearl did can't be too bad. I mean, the building is still standing, and we're open for business, right?"

"I love your positive attitude." I turned my gaze to the overhead monitors above the cashier counter. Cherise appeared on screen. She flipped the *Come in, We're Open* sign to the reverse side, which read *"Closed – Will Return"*. She moved the shorter of the two plastic clock hands forward 15 minutes and twisted the sign back so that the clock face displayed outward.

The Gas N'Go's security camera was an older model with fuzzy resolution, but the quality was good enough to identify Cherise, or anyone else who passed near or through the front door.

I felt a pang of guilt for incriminating Aunt Pearl, but if my hunch was right, I would have plenty of time to clear things up later.

"Cherise, what time did you start work today?"

"Seven a.m., like usual. This is my first shift in four days. Follow me."

I trailed behind Cherise as we headed down a narrow hallway to the back of the store.

Cherise opened the door to a small room. Dusty moving boxes were stacked up against one wall underneath a large calendar that was two years out of date.

An ancient-looking oak desk was covered with stacks of old magazines and papers. Behind it was a green leather upholstered office chair. The armrests were worn and ripped. What remained was held together with duct tape.

"Just show me where I can see the security camera footage and I'll let you get back to work. I'll be quick, I promise." I fondled the flash drive in my jacket pocket, hoping that this wasn't just a fruitless exercise. I also hoped to find something, because the alternative—that Steve had died as a result of curse housekeeping negligence—was a catastrophic tragedy.

Cherise sat down and reached for the handle of the bottom desk drawer. She pulled a laptop from the drawer and set it down on the desk. She powered it on and typed onto the keyboard. The screen brightened and filled with surveillance footage of the Gas N'Go front door. She pointed to up and down arrows at the bottom of the screen. "Click the menu at the top to switch from one camera to another. Come and get me if you need help navigating."

"Thanks, Cherise." I didn't look up. I was already scrolling through footage.

Cherise's footsteps faded down the hallway as she headed back to the front of the store.

I pulled the soggy receipt from my pocket and carefully flattened it on the desktop. The receipt had a time and date stamp, but all I could decipher from the faded ink was yesterday's date. I decided to start my search at opening time yesterday, 7 a.m. I scrolled back until I saw movement on the screen. Cherise's back faced me as she unlocked the front door and switched the sign to the blue side that said, *'Come In, We're Open'*.

I scrolled slowly through each frame, stopping each time a figure darkened the doorway. There was no sound. It was like watching a very boring silent movie. A few dozen customers came and went: local men and women, and a couple of kids. Tyler was one of them. I froze the frame for a moment to admire my tall, muscular boyfriend looking handsome in his sheriff's uniform.

Cherise came out from behind the counter and offered Tyler the same tray of chocolate samples she had offered me. He declined with an apologetic smile before heading to the rear of the store, out of camera range. Moments later he returned to the cashier, a coffee and muffin in hand. He paid for his purchases and exited the store a few minutes later.

She was really pushing those chocolates!

Cherise had worked yesterday despite claiming not to. Why had she lied about today being her first shift after four days off? She couldn't possibly have forgotten. Whatever her reason was for lying, it couldn't be serious. After all, she had allowed me to review the surveillance footage, knowing I would see her on camera.

There was a small uptick in activity around noon that soon petered out. Minutes came and went with nobody entering or leaving the store, and nothing at all happened. I began to doubt whether I was on the right track at all.

An hour went by with no customers. Then, just after 3 o'clock, two teen boys burst into the store, laughing and joking. The Puhl brothers each bought soft drinks and potato chips and left a few minutes later.

The store became quiet again, the start of yet another lull with no customers or deliveries. Cherise sat at the counter and read magazines. A 12-hour shift wasn't as bad as it sounded, given all the downtime in between customers. How the Gas N'Go managed to stay in business was a mystery, but the cameras provided undeniable proof that those chocolates hadn't 'just arrived' this morning as Cherise had claimed.

I had almost given up when a shadowy figure darkened

the door and pulled it open. It was almost 7 p.m., according to the time stamp on the video, just minutes from closing time.

A shiver went down my spine as I squinted at the screen. The man looked like a would-be robber rather than a customer, dressed in dark clothing with a black hoodie pulled up to partially obscure his face. He looked down as if trying to avoid detection or recognition, like a practiced burglar.

He glanced nervously around the store, then lowered his gaze as if he didn't want to be noticed. He strode to the back of the store, out of camera range. He moved quickly, as if in a hurry. About all I could tell from the footage was that this man didn't want to interact or be remembered. He looked to be up to no good, though from that particular camera angle I couldn't see much.

I switched to the camera facing the front counter, going back to opening time yesterday. I scrolled through the footage at double speed, watching the same customers as before, only this time I focused on each person as they paid Cherise for their purchases.

Cherise made small talk with each customer and never failed to push the Valentine's Day chocolate. I was still troubled by her claim that she hadn't worked yesterday. What possible reason could she have for lying?

I slowed the film down to normal speed and watched Cherise joke with a couple buying lottery tickets. She tried to upsell them on the same valentine chocolate box she had offered to me, and then scolded the Puhl boys for too many refills at the Slurpee machine.

At 6:58 p.m., just minutes before closing time, the

mystery man brought his purchases up to the counter. The largest item was white, large, and rectangular in shape, but because of the video's poor resolution, it was hard to make out any more detail. The packaging was bigger than most food items likely to be sold in a convenience store. Judging from the way the man lifted it onto the counter, it was also heavy.

Cherise didn't attempt to move the item. Instead, she turned it around and took aim at it with her bar code scanner. She scanned the remaining two items with her hand-held scanner. I couldn't make out the two smaller items, but this was the only customer who had bought three items all day.

Cherise held a finger to her mouth and smiled as she said something to the man on the silent film. I couldn't tell if he answered since his back was to the camera. He pulled out his wallet and extracted a wad of bills. He peeled off three of them with a gloved hand and handed them to Cherise. He then pulled a large black bag from his jacket pocket and placed the items inside. That struck me as unusual, since men rarely carried reusable bags in their pockets. Most people also removed their gloves when entering a store, especially when paying for their purchases. This man seemed intent on covering his tracks.

Cherise dropped loose change into the man's gloved palm. He shoved the coins into his pants pocket. He turned and exited the store with his bulky purchase, one hand supporting the bag underneath.

The mystery item was heavy and awkward judging by the way the man carried it. Whatever it was, it was heavy enough to kill someone. Could this have been one of the items on the receipt? This receipt had to belong to the man. None of the other customers had bought three items. I wished I could tell what those three items were. I zoomed in on the footage frame by frame, but the low-resolution images only blurred the more I enlarged them.

I didn't want to alert Cherise to my real reason for reviewing the surveillance footage, so I couldn't ask her what the items were. Then I had an idea. It would be hard to identify the smaller items, but there weren't too many large items in the store. I remembered that the man had gone to the back of the store first.

I walked back out to the store where Cherise caught my eye.

"Just checking something, but I'm not finished yet," I said.

She nodded and returned to reading her magazine.

I walked down each of the three aisles and along the perimeter of the store, looking for an item that was heavy, square, and large.

I returned to the office and advanced the video frame by frame to review it one more time. My heart raced as I pressed pause. I pulled my phone from my pocket and called Tyler. "Meet me at your office. I think I just found the murder weapon."

After making arrangements to meet him, I pulled a flash drive from my purse and copied the video files. Once finished, I carefully placed the flash drive into the zippered pocket of my purse. I noted the time on the tape before rewinding it to the beginning. I didn't want Cherise or anyone else knowing what I had seen until I could make sense of it myself.

CHAPTER 23

Ten minutes later we sat in Tyler's police precinct office, our chairs squeezed together in front of his computer screen. I pulled my flash drive from my pocket and inserted it into the computer. I scrolled through the Gas N'Go video footage until the man in black walked through the front door.

"It's not the best resolution, but do you recognize that guy?" I pointed at the screen.

Tyler squinted. "Isn't that Jason McCoy?"

"It is. I didn't recognize him at first, but I guess famous people go incognito to avoid being noticed. He bought ice." The details that had been hard to see on the old Gas N'Go monitor were much clearer on the police station's larger screen.

Tyler's face flushed. "Ice?"

My face flushed as I remembered what else was sometimes called ice. Ice was a slang word for diamonds. Had Tyler noticed the ring missing yet?

"Ice is a heavy enough to kill someone."

"He probably just bought the ice for drinks. He picked up a few items shortly after they checked in, for snacks and so on. The most logical reason is the likely one."

I cleared my throat. "Except that it's block ice. Crushed ice I get—people use it for drinks. Who needs a block of ice in the dead of winter?"

"Inventory doesn't exactly fly off the shelves at the Gas N'Go," Tyler said. "Maybe the store ran out of crushed ice. Block ice was all that was left."

We watched Jason pay for his purchase and turn toward the door. He disappeared from the camera. I stopped the film and clicked onto the door camera. Jason reappeared. He walked to the door, pausing to balance the heavy, cold block of ice as he opened the door. His Porsche was visible outside, parked at the closest gas pump.

I flashed back to Cherise and Jason at the cash. Jason had been dressed to avoid recognition, but Cherise must have recognized him. She had brought her finger to her lips to let Jason know that she would keep his secret. Since the footage had no audio, I couldn't know for sure, but not outing a celebrity made sense. It could also explain why Cherise had lied about not working yesterday. She was afraid of betraying Jason McCoy's secret visit to our little town.

I extracted the receipt from my purse and handed it to Tyler. "I found this under the pool hedge. It's probably Jason's receipt since he was the only customer to buy three items yesterday. I don't know what the other two items are. It may not really matter in the end."

Tyler frowned. "I'll find out. How did the Shady Creek police miss that receipt? They were all over that place."

I didn't have the greatest confidence in the Shady Creek police myself, but missing a receipt seemed unlikely. "Maybe the wind blew it there later? The forensics team were already under the impression it was an accident, not a murder. It could have affected the thoroughness of their search."

"It's disappointing and I'm going to have to talk to them about it," Tyler said. "Serena never mentioned the gas station. She claimed they all went straight to the Rocklin mansion and stayed there."

I tapped the screen. "Maybe she sent Jason out for some things once they arrived and forgot about it."

Tyler sighed. "I suppose."

"The ice really is weird, Tyler. People substitute crushed ice when block ice is unavailable to use in their cooler on a summer camping or fishing trip. Nobody gets block ice for their drinks when crushed ice isn't available."

Tyler pondered that for a moment. "Okay, so Jason bought this block of ice, and yet we found no ice at the house. They could have used the ice for something already."

I swallowed hard at the mention of missing ice. I had to find that ring. "They didn't use it for drinks."

"We didn't see any ice in the freezer. We did a pretty thorough search of the house and grounds too. Both freezers were empty as I recall."

"Yet Steve died from blunt force trauma and a block of ice carries a lot of blunt force." I pressed play again and we both watched Jason exit the store. "See how he's carrying it? It wasn't so much the weight of the ice that made him uncomfortable. It's because it's freezing cold. That's probably why he wore gloves, aside from not wanting to leave any fingerprints anywhere. He's holding the block of ice up against his side, because ice is awkward and heavy to carry."

Tyler's mouth dropped open. "It's the perfect murder weapon. It's heavy enough to kill, yet it leaves no trace. It explains the bruising on Steve's temple, yet it melted before we could find it."

"How long does it take to melt a block of ice?" I asked.

It was more of a statement, but Tyler took it as a question. "Outside, in the freezing cold, it could take a while, even in a heated pool. It all depends on the pool temperature settings."

"Or it could be done even quicker under a hot water tap or in the microwave," I said.

Tyler nodded. "It's a definite possibility. It's still a really tight timeline, considering the short difference in time between when you and Ruby last saw Steve alive, and when Ruby discovered the body."

I nodded. "I think the ice was left in the pool to melt and disappear. It explains the uneven temperature I felt when I stuck my hand in the water. It was really cold in a couple of places. And there were bits of ice floating on the surface, yet it was a heated pool. I had thought that the water was freezing over due to the cold, but now I'm thinking it was just leftover ice. The bigger bits could have been removed and taken inside and disposed of down a sink drain, or a toilet flush.

"You stuck your hand in the water? At a crime scene? Cen!"

I held up my palms. "Sorry. Aunt Pearl accidentally dropped your jacket in the water. Actually, only part of the jacket fell in. I knew I had to get it out."

Tyler's eyes widened as he reached for his right-hand jacket pocket. His mouth dropped open when he realized the pocket was empty and he was wearing a different jacket. "The jacket in the backseat of my car? Where is that jacket, exactly?"

My pulse quickened as I thought about the engagement ring that had been in his pocket. "Uh…don't worry, it's safe. Last I saw it was at the inn, hanging on a coat hook in the hall to dry out."

Our eyes met.

His eyes searched mine, probably wondering if I knew about the ring.

It was hard, but I kept my face expressionless. "What's wrong?"

He frowned. "Never mind."

My face flushed as I broke his gaze. I swallowed hard and changed the subject back to the McCoys. "The McCoys are out for dinner right now, but what if they check out early upon their return? We'd better get back to the mansion."

"You're right, let's go. Call Ruby and ask her to meet us there with keys so we can get inside."

CHAPTER 24

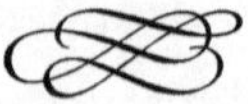

When Tyler and I returned to the Rocklin mansion, Mom and Aunt Pearl were already waiting by the front door. Grandma Vi was there too, floating above them and bragging about me lifting the curse.

"I don't believe you. Prove it." Aunt Pearl stared up at Grandma Vi, who hovered about five feet overhead.

It was quite confusing to Tyler, who couldn't see or hear ghostly Grandma Vi's part of the conversation. He whispered, "Why is Pearl talking to herself?"

"I'll explain later." I motioned for Mom to unlock the door as I grabbed Tyler's arm and steered him to the house.

Aunt Pearl stormed toward us. "You shouldn't have risked coming here, Cendrine. You think you canceled the curse but instead you just made things worse. We don't need any more accidents, and we should leave now while we can."

Mom ignored her and turned the key in the door lock. She motioned to Tyler to open it.

"Cut the chit chat." Tyler turned the doorknob and opened the front door. He ushered us inside into a dark hallway. I entered first, followed by Mom and Aunt Pearl. Mom switched on the hall lights. Tyler closed the door and fell in behind me as I walked down the hallway.

"Why are we going to the kitchen?" Mom asked. "Everything happened outside."

Even Tyler seemed sceptical all of a sudden. "Cen has a theory."

"Of course, she does," Aunt Pearl muttered. "Cen thinks she's smarter than the rest of us."

"I'm pretty sure I've found something." I walked to the rear of the large kitchen and pointed at the closed pantry door. I just hoped I wasn't too late. "Open this for me, please."

Tyler pulled a pair of latex gloves from his jacket pocket and put them on. He carefully turned the doorknob. The door opened into a long room with floor-to-ceiling cupboards on one side and open shelves on the other. At the far end of the room was a large upright freezer. It was stainless steel with two side-by-side doors and a deep drawer on the bottom.

Aunt Pearl eyed the spacious pantry. "Wow, Ruby, you sure went overboard with the appliances. Granite countertops in the pantry are a bit much, don't you think?"

Mom sighed. "Can't you just be nice for a change?"

Tyler pursed his lips. "Okay, now what?"

I pointed at the refrigerator. "Open it, please."

He opened one refrigerator door and then the other.

They were empty. He bent down and opened the bottom freezer drawer and pulled out a gallon-sized container of ice cream. It was a value-priced brand, the one carried by the Gas N'Go. It was the only item in the freezer, and I knew the price of that discount ice cream was about the same as item 2 on the Gas N'Go receipt.

I felt a surge of relief that my hunch had proved correct about item 2 on the receipt.

"What does a container of chocolate ice cream have to do with anything?" Mom asked. "You're not seriously going to eat their chocolate ice cream, are you? They haven't even left yet."

"Just bear with me, Mom." I turned to Tyler. "Bring that into the kitchen and I'll grab a spoon."

We followed Tyler out of the pantry and into the kitchen.

Aunt Pearl said, "She's already blown her diet, so she's decided to binge on a feeding frenzy."

Mom frowned. "Seriously, Cen, you can eat all the ice cream you want at home."

Aunt Pearl had to get in the last word in. "Hah! You're weak! I knew you had zero willpower."

I ignored them as I walked toward the kitchen island.

Aunt Pearl was persistent. "Cen's got a death wish, Ruby. The longer we spend here the more danger we're in. We really need to get out of here before something terrible happens."

I kept my voice calm, though I was losing patience. "I already told you, the curse has been taken care of."

"What are you talk—?" Tyler stopped mid-sentence as he thought better of baiting Aunt Pearl. He placed the ice cream carton on the marble countertop of the kitchen island and looked at me.

"Nothing's going to happen to any of us. Gloves?" I held out my palm.

Tyler pulled a pair of latex gloves from his pocket and handed them to me. I pulled them on, then searched the drawers and cupboards until I found an ice cream scoop and a large bowl.

Aunt Pearl shook her head. "You're acting like a lunatic, Cendrine. The curse has made you lose your mind."

"I found a receipt from the Gas 'N Go for a few items bought last night just before closing. Jason McCoy bought a block of ice, a one-gallon container of chocolate ice cream, and one other item I can't identify. Do you see a block of ice in this freezer?"

"No, but it isn't the only freezer in the house," Mom pointed to the kitchen refrigerator, a smaller version of the one in the pantry. "The bottom fridge drawer is a freezer."

Tyler walked over to the fridge and opened the drawer. It was completely empty except for a tray of ice cubes. He closed it. "No block of ice there."

"Who cares? Maybe they already used it." Aunt Pearl tapped her foot impatiently. "Can we go now?"

"I can see buying ice cubes for drinks," Mom said. "But a block of ice in midwinter doesn't make much sense. It's February and freezing outside."

"Exactly." I set the ice cream container down on the kitchen island and carefully removed the lid with my gloved hand. I turned the container sideways so that we could all see the contents.

The chocolate ice cream was smooth and untouched

with no signs of scoop marking the chocolate ice cream. It was still full but there was one unusual feature. It had a coating of hoary frost, as if the ice cream had partially melted and refrozen again.

I began scooping ice cream from the container and dropped the scoops into the bowl. "We really need to get to the bottom of this."

Aunt Pearl stomped her foot. "Take your gluttonous appetite elsewhere, Cendrine! You are not eating anything in this cursed house!"

I ignored her and continued scooping ice cream from the carton and placing it into the bowl. I was halfway down the container now, the fingertips of my gloves coated in a chocolatey ice glaze. I scooped faster and faster until the ice cream scoop caught onto something at the bottom of the container.

Beneath all the ice cream was plastic with blue and white writing. I scraped away at it, slowly uncovering it enough to read the lettering. The plastic bag that had once held a block of ice was neatly folded on the bottom of the ice cream tub. The thrill of the reveal was just like uncovering a Kinder Surprise egg prize or a trinket from a Cracker Jack box.

I held up the almost empty container. "Evidence of the murder weapon, or at least the bag it came in."

Mom's mouth formed an 'O' as realization dawned. "Steve got iced with a block of ice?"

I nodded and turned to Aunt Pearl. "Remember how the pool had hot and cold spots when you put your hand in it?"

Tyler's eyes widened in shock. "Pearl's hand was in the pool too?"

"Tattle tale," Aunt Pearl snapped. "Cen did exactly the same thing when she was trying to find the ri—"

I lunged forward and cupped my hand over Aunt Pearl's mouth. "We both tried to grab your jacket, and everything's fine now."

Tyler eyed us suspiciously. "What's going on between you two?"

"Not important right now," I said. "The killer hit Steven over the head with a block of ice. The killer melted the murder weapon, leaving no trace in the pool other than a few small bits of ice floating on the surface that we all mistook for surface frost."

Tyler pulled his phone from his pocket and walked over to the window. He relayed our findings to the ME and asked her if Steve's head injury fit the profile of a block of ice. A few minutes later he returned. "She said the murder weapon idea fits."

Tyler walked a few feet away to continue his call with the ME in private.

Mom smiled. "You're brilliant, Cen. The murder weapon melted, leaving no fingerprints or forensics. One thing I don't get—wouldn't it take forever for a block of ice to melt? The temperature outside is freezing. How could anything melt in winter?"

"The pool is heated." I pointed out. "In fact, the heat was turned up to the max. Steven had adjusted the temperature beforehand, so that it was warm enough to swim in. All the killer had to do was turn up the pool temperature even further to the maximum. You're right though. It would take a while to melt a very big block of ice, probably fifteen or twenty minutes at least. What we found in the pool were probably just ice fragments. Remember when you saw the kitchen tap still running, Mom? I think the block of ice was melted there under hot water. The evidence literally went down the drain."

CHAPTER 25

Tyler finished his call and strolled back into the kitchen.

"The killer had to be as tall as Steve to hit him on the head," Mom said to him. "Stronger than me, because I certainly can't lift a block of ice over my head. Have you ruled me out yet, Sheriff?"

"I can't confirm or deny, Ruby," Tyler said. "But you're right. Someone quite strong killed Steve. It's likely a man."

"Jason argued with Steve just before he died," Mom said. "Jason was also fired from the show too."

"It could also be Lucky," I explained what I had overheard Lucky and Jason discussing at The Witching Post. "He was talking about a job with Jason. I'm guessing Jason wanted to hire him for something other than bartending."

Aunt Pearl shook her head. "Why do you have it in for him? Lucky was working and you know it, Cen."

"I'm just exploring all possibilities, and their conversation was suspicious given Steve's death shortly after," I said. "The killer knew Steve's habits, and that he would be swimming in the pool. It could be someone close to Steve, or it could be someone close who hired someone."

"Everyone knows Steve and his habits from the reality show," Aunt Pearl pointed out.

Mom frowned. "That's true, but his swim workouts were new. He told Cen and me that his swim workouts had started in January as a New Year's resolution. They planned to reveal it on a future episode, but he's never talked about swimming on the show. I know, because I've seen every episode."

Mom's Real McCoys obsession was worse than I thought. However, her statement only confirmed that the killer had information known only to a few.

"Ruby has a point. Only people in his inner circle know that he swims," Tyler said.

I said, "The killer followed Steve to the pool and hit him in the head with the ice block just as he reached the pool edge. When Steve struggled, the attacker hit him repeatedly until Steve died. The killer pushed his body into the pool."

Mom gasped. "The perfect murder with a murder weapon that melts."

Aunt Pearl scowled. "That's so far-fetched that it's unbelievable. Why weren't there any footprints? Because it's a curse, that's why."

"There's a simple explanation," I said. "The killer poured hot water on the patio to erase his tracks as he walked back into the house."

Aunt Pearl shook her head. "Your theories get crazier by

the minute, Cendrine. You and Ruby's greedy get-rich-quick schemes will ruin us all."

Mom rolled her eyes but kept silent.

It was hard to ignore Aunt Pearl but I pressed on.

"The killer still had to dispose of the bag the ice came in. Who would look in an ice cream container full of ice cream? Nobody, it turns out. Not even the Shady Creek investigators. The killer transferred the ice cream to another container like I did just now. He stuck it in the microwave to liquify it. He placed the empty block ice bag into the bottom of the ice cream container, and then poured the melted ice cream back into the ice cream container to cover the bag. He placed the ice cream back into the freezer to refreeze."

"Is there a way to know who came and went from here?" Mom asked.

"There are cameras, but unfortunately the camera at the entrance gate was shut off," Tyler said. "Which also points to it being an inside job. Somebody planned this. Whoever killed Steve had the foresight to turn off that camera, but not the other ones."

"What about the other cameras?" Mom asked.

Tyler shook his head. "They didn't record any activity either. Unfortunately, they don't cover all parts of the property, and not all of the cameras were in working order. It's quite possible that someone came and went but evaded detection. In fact, that has to be the case since we haven't found any intruders on the footage."

"No cameras in the pool area?" I asked. "Surely there was one at the pool gate."

Tyler shook his head. "Sorry, no."

Aunt Pearl stomped her foot in frustration. She shook a finger at Mom. "Your cameras don't even work. Your sloppy magic has ruined us forever, Ruby."

Mom flushed with anger. "My 'sloppy magic' pays the mortgage, Pearl."

Aunt Pearl ranted on. "You're ruining our reputation, and you're driving away student witches from Pearl's Charm School. We're never going to recover."

Tyler stepped in between Mom and Aunt Pearl and extended his arms palms out. "Stop arguing and focus. The front gate camera would have been helpful, but there are other ways to determine who was and wasn't here."

"Well then, Sheriff. Hurry up and tell us." Aunt Pearl crossed her arms and tapped her foot. "I'm waiting."

Tyler took a deep breath. "It's true that only a few people are strong enough and tall enough to kill Steve. It's also true that a small number of people had the motive and opportunity to kill Steve. For the moment, let's focus on motive only. Who benefits from Steve's death?"

"Jason was mad at being cut from the show, plus he has an expensive drug habit," Mom said. "It's got to be him."

"Why kill only Steve and not Serena too?" I asked.

"He was probably going to kill her next," Mom said.

"Possible," said Tyler. "Though I think he'd want to get it over with as soon as possible. He would have waited until they were alone there together and killed them both. You could have been killed too, because you almost certainly interrupted the killer. I think that is who you were talking to. Can you remember the voice clearly? Could Steve's impersonator have been Jason, for instance?"

"I-I'm not sure. I was listening to the words, not the voice so much," Mom said.

"I don't think it's Jason," Tyler said. "He would be more likely to steal from them, so killing them is like killing the golden goose. No matter how mad he is, he has no one else. He's financially dependent on them, and because of that, the Real McCoys continues to provide an income. That income evaporates with Steve gone. Anyone on the crew has the same disincentive."

"When I overheard Jason and Lucky talking, it sure sounded like Jason wanted to hire him to do something shady," I said. "Also, Lucky was on the property here right after Steve's death. He was supposed to be tending bar at the Witching Post, but I'm not sure when he left."

"Lucky would be doing it for Jason though," Tyler said. "The end result is the same: Jason's cashflow dries up."

"It could be a love triangle," I said. "Maybe Serena wanted Steve out of the way."

"But without Steve, the show would be canceled," Mom said.

"Not if she got another co-star," I said. "It's a reality show that feeds on conflict. It's like all-star wrestling. It's all a show for entertainment purposes. All you need is someone willing to play the game. Someone who will do outrageous things, play off Serena's character, someone who will defer to Serena, someone who's attractive, who was as interesting as Steve. Someone like—"

"Danny Nastasio!" Mom and Aunt Pearl said in unison.

"Did you see the how that man looked at her?" Mom exclaimed. "I wish a man looked at me like that."

Aunt Pearl nodded. "I'm betting he does a lot more than

drive her car. Their story about shopping at Bunny's Key to Fashion is just ridiculous. Who could seriously spend 45 minutes in Bunny's store? That was just to manufacture an alibi."

My mouth dropped open, shocked by Aunt Pearl's abrupt change of opinion.

Tyler bit his lip. "It makes a lot of sense. A divorce threatens the continued running of the show since it's about a married couple. In addition, Serena would have to split everything financial with Steve. If Serena is widowed, then she inherits Steve's half and probably gets a nice insurance settlement too."

I nodded. "Bunny's alibi isn't all that reliable because of her failing memory, but what about Abby, Danny, and Serena alibiing each other? They corroborate each other, but what if it's a cover-up for murder?" I had an idea, but I needed Tyler's help to prove it.

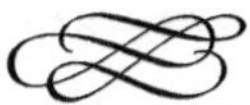

CHAPTER 26

Tyler called the Shady Creek Police to keep surveillance on Serena and her entourage as they dined at an upscale restaurant in Shady Creek. The police had instructions to delay their departure for at least an hour. In the meantime, Tyler and I sat in his office and reviewed security camera footage from outside Bunny's Key to Fashion and the nearby café.

It was clear from Bunny's camera that Serena's Mercedes had never left its parking spot outside the clothing store, giving the two women what appeared to be an airtight alibi. Whether anyone came or went from the Mercedes wasn't clear though, since only the rear of the SUV was captured on camera.

Tyler had obtained security footage from neighboring businesses. He brought the footage up on the screen, one camera at a time. He scanned through several cameras but found nothing of consequence. Serena and Abby were seen entering the store. The Mercedes never moved from its parking spot. There were three businesses with security cameras that captured movement in and around Bunny's store. None of them showed anything other than Serena and Abby entering the store, and their departure almost two hours later.

It was hard to shop for any longer than about ten minutes at Bunny's Key to Fashion. Two hours was an eternity to browse in the tiny store. Even allowing for chit-chat with Bunny, they should have been out of there in twenty minutes.

There were four more stores with security cameras, but they didn't face the store. Tyler sped up the playback as we scanned each one. It was tedious work, even with the playback sped up.

Thirty minutes later, Tyler clicked on the footage from the security camera outside Molly's Café and Bistro. The cafe was just off Main Street and around the corner from Bunny's store. It was in the general proximity of the store, but it offered no view of the store itself.

There were several vehicles parked on the street, among them a white van parked right outside the café. The van caught my eye because it was a current-year model. Most people in our not-so-prosperous town drove cars that were at least ten years old, so the white van really stood out.

I tapped the screen. "Can you pause and zoom in? That van looks just like one of the Real McCoys vans parked at our inn."

Tyler zoomed in on the van's license plate, which was out of state. He jotted down the plate number before stepping away to another desk. Moments later, he returned.

"You're right, Cen. Those plates are registered to the McCoy's film production company."

Tyler restarted the footage. A minute later, the van pulled out of the parking spot outside the café. It turned the corner onto Main Street and disappeared from view.

We watched the empty parking spot stay empty as the camera advanced.

"Can we go back earlier to see when the van was parked?" I hoped to catch a glimpse of the driver.

Tyler shook his head. "This particular camera started right here, with the van already parked. It's on a loop that constantly rerecords new footage on top of old every 24 hours. We've still got a few more cameras to review. Maybe something else will turn up."

"That means that the driver was already in the driver's seat at 10:30 a.m., when the camera started rolling." I was disappointed that I was unable to see anyone getting into the van. People walked back and forth on the sidewalk, but the parking spot remained empty for what seemed like an eternity.

Suddenly the white van returned, parking in the same spot in front of the café.

"It's back!" Tyler said. "It's been gone almost two hours. If course, there could be a logical explanation for that."

"Depends who's driving," I said.

Everyone had been so fixated on the Mercedes to corroborate their alibis, that the movements of other vehicles weren't closely scrutinized. Until now.

"Can you zoom in on the windows, Tyler?"

He increased the magnification. "It's too grainy to see anything, especially from the passenger side. There's someone in the driver's seat—obviously—since that person just parked the van. Any one of the crew could have a valid reason for being there, but it's awfully coincidental."

"He's probably going to get out of the van," I said. "But this view is from the passenger side. Is there another camera angle from across the street?"

"Already on it." Tyler clicked on another file and we saw the café from the vantage point that captured the van's driver's side. Soon a tall man exited the van. He wore a baseball cap low over his eyes and a bulky dark-colored jacket. Both the shadow of the buildings and the brim of his cap made his face dark and hard to identify. He walked briskly to the corner before disappearing from view.

He was headed in the direction of Bunny's store. "Look how he holds his arms up high as he walks. It's a very distinctive stride. I think it's Danny Nastasio."

Tyler enlarged the image. "His build looks similar too. Danny claimed to have been parked outside of Bunny's the entire time, so if you're right, there goes his alibi. He could have driven the van to just outside the Rocklin place and walked onto the property undetected. He kills Steve, runs back to the van and drives back to repark the van and walk back to the Mercedes. I'll follow up with more stores to see if there's any security camera footage we missed. I'll also get the Shady Creek forensics back here to collect fingerprints and DNA off the ice cream container and the block ice package. I wouldn't expect Danny's fingerprints or DNA to be on it, since we know that Jason bought it. Unless Danny served the ice cream or put away the groceries, that is. I'll get the forensics team to collect DNA from the Shady Creek restaurant where they're dining right now. The DNA will take some time to confirm, but hopefully the fingerprints will give us preliminary confirmation that's enough to take this a step further.

Tyler's phone buzzed. He glanced at it and then back at me. "I've got to take this—it's the ME."

I nodded and refocused on the screen. There had to be something more definitive on camera. A good lawyer could probably explain away the fingerprints and DNA, and if they did, then there was no case. Even if the ME changed her mind on the cause of death, it would be an uphill battle to press charges on just circumstantial evidence.

Serena would add to the pressure. The Real McCoys reality show had tens of millions of viewers. Like it or not, such a huge fanbase could potentially influence whether charges were laid and what those charges were. Steve's death would be explained on the show, a show that was watched by millions. Serena would control the narrative, and the evidence otherwise would have to be pretty convincing.

I zoomed in on the van again, hoping to see something we had missed earlier. The bright sunshine made it impossible to see the van's interior. But the van driver was somehow involved with the McCoys since the van was registered to them. The driver was an out-of-towner, someone locals might remember seeing.

Tyler raced back into the room, breathless. "Grab your coat, you're coming with me."

What he said next changed everything.

CHAPTER 27

"The medical examiner has now officially changed the cause of death from undetermined to homicide from blunt force trauma, based on the ice block evidence. She confirmed that the size and shape match the blunt force trauma on Steve's head."

The snowflakes turned from flurries to heavy snow as we sped toward Shady Creek. The Shady Creek police were waiting for Tyler's arrival. Once that happened, Serena, Jason, Danny, and Abby would be asked to visit the precinct and provide statements about the newly uncovered evidence. The Jeep's tires slipped on the unplowed road as we rounded a turn in the road.

I grabbed the door handle to steady myself as we skidded. "Slow down, Tyler. They aren't going anywhere."

He frowned and turned to me. "Don't be so sure. Someone tipped them off that we were at the house. The undercover officer seated at the next table overheard them debating whether to even return tonight. They're all a flight risk. Serena's talking about chartering a flight out. In fact, Abby's calling some local charter companies right now."

The restaurant was a half mile from the interstate and an equal distance to the regional airport. We were twenty miles away on a rural road, unlucky to catch them in time.

"Can't the Shady Creek police detain them?"

"They can't detain a group of people without good reason. Not without arresting them."

"Do you really think anyone will fly in this weather?" The Shady Creek airport usually shuts down in stormy weather.

"I sure hope not, Cen, but with money somebody will probably fly them out. Serena's also been talking to her lawyer about an accidental death lawsuit. She wants to sue Ruby as well as the town. Westwick Corners doesn't have the funds to fight a lawsuit. We'd have to settle, and that would bankrupt the town."

"She's using the lawsuit as a distraction technique," I said. "It's a scare tactic so you don't pursue any angle other than accidental death."

"It's not going to work," Tyler said. "Her behavior is definitely incriminating for a grieving spouse. Why would she even consider protecting anyone who could potentially have killed her husband?"

I nodded. "I don't think Jason killed Steve. I don't think for a minute that Serena, his stepmom, would financially support him once Steve was gone, and I believe Jason knows that. Serena wouldn't protect him either."

"You think someone asked Jason to buy the ice?"

I nodded. "I do. The only people that can order Jason

around are either Serena or Steve. One of them probably asked him to pick up a few things at the store."

"But his time was unaccounted for, and you saw his car gone from the Witching Post parking lot."

"Yes," I agreed. "But I had seen him in the bar only minutes earlier. That wouldn't have left enough time to kill Steve, melt the ice and hide the bag in the freezer. He seems the obvious suspect, but I suspect he's being framed."

"You think Serena—?"

I nodded. "Danny Nastasio is much more than just a loyal employee. I think he's romantically involved with Serena. Did you notice the way he looks at her? I mean, she is beautiful, but it's more than that."

"You think he's in love with her?" Tyler asked.

"Isn't it obvious? The way he's always around, but unlike Abby, he just stays in the background so as to not draw attention to himself. He's the odd man out in a love triangle, and he's fed up. It's a powerful motive for murder."

Tyler nodded. "A jealous lover. But he has less to gain than Serena. With Steve gone, she doesn't have to get divorced. She probably wanted out of the relationship without the financial hit. No custody battle though. They don't have any children together."

"No children, but their reality show is kind of their baby, since they started it together from nothing and grew it into a multi-million-dollar empire. They could have disagreed on the show's direction, intellectual property, or merchandising. It wouldn't be the first time. I know that Steve objected to Jason being written out of the show, but it happened anyway. He eventually went along with it, but Serena calls the shots.

"Also, Abby let it slip that Steve was being written out of the show next year. I can't imagine him quitting voluntarily. That show was pretty much a gravy train for both of them. Why else would he say his swim workouts were going to be part of next season's show? There's no question that Serena's more popular than Steve, but she still needed him as a sidekick to balance her psycho behavior. People tune in each week because they're addicted to seeing their dysfunctional relationship."

"That would make his murder premeditated," Tyler said. "If Serena already had Steve written out of the show because she knew he'd be dead by next season, that's pretty incriminating. I wonder if his swim workouts were her idea or his? Maybe we can find a script that proves it. The more evidence we have, the stronger the case."

As we pulled into the restaurant parking lot, I was relieved to see the white Mercedes still parked outside. I also couldn't help but notice an unmarked police car parked opposite, with two undercover cops inside.

CHAPTER 28

The busy diner's conversational hum suddenly went quiet. People turned toward the raised voices. Some recognized the star in their midst. Two others, I realized were two more undercover cops. The man and woman, both in their early thirties and fit-looking, sat across the aisle, one booth back. They were ready to spring into action at a moment's notice.

"You're all crazy!" Serena swore. "The producers wrote Steve out of the show because he's been very erratic lately. It was getting harder and harder to film each episode without Steve flying off the handle. Tell them, Abby."

Abby bit her lip, clearly uncomfortable with Serena's request. "I know that the script got changed last week. Steve was going to be replaced with a new co-star."

I frowned. "A new co-star? It's a reality show about marriage. Why did you want us to arrange the vow renewals, then?"

Abby shrugged. "It's confidential. I can't tell you any more than that."

Serena rolled her eyes. "The Real McCoys is just a show about love and all its ups and downs, and we wanted to retire at the top of our game. This was part of scaling back, and it involved writing the final chapters of our on-screen relationship. That's got nothing to do with our real-life relationship. Just because it's a reality show doesn't mean that it follows our lives exactly. We're too boring in real life. You saw us, Cen. Would you watch that for entertainment?"

I flashed back to our earlier meeting with Serena, Steve, and Mom. They had seemed the perfect couple, but actors were good at make-believe. "No, of course not."

"Glad we've got that cleared up. You traveled all this way in a snowstorm for nothing." Serena turned to Abby. "Book us hotel rooms here for the night."

The undercover officer who had been seated nearby rose from his seat and walked to the door. Just then a twenty-something waitress appeared with the check and an autograph request.

Danny stood and walked over to wait by Serena as she rummaged through her purse. He crossed his arms and watched us, his face expressionless.

I was sure more than ever that he was the van driver. His height and bodybuilder build were unique. He towered over Tyler by a few inches, and it was his muscular arms that gave him the distinctive stride with his arms held high.

Serena dropped her credit card on the table and signed a napkin for the waitress.

"Where's Steve?" the waitress asked. "I'd like his autograph too."

After a few seconds of silence, Serena answered. "He's indisposed, so I'm afraid you're out of luck. Whatever you heard here, you have to promise that you won't breathe a word."

She dropped three hundred-dollar bills on the table and stood. "Keep the change. Abby, did you get a hotel yet?"

"That won't be necessary," Tyler said. "You're all coming with me."

* * *

TEN MINUTES LATER, Serena, Abby, and Danny sat in separate interview rooms at the Shady Creek Police precinct. Serena broke first. She claimed that Danny killed Steve in a drunken rage and that he had threatened her too. When that didn't work, she bargained with Tyler, offering to drop her accidental death lawsuit if Tyler would drop the investigation. He didn't.

I sat in another room and watched Danny's interrogation unfold on camera. Tyler and a Shady Creek detective pulled their chairs closer to Danny. Tyler did the talking. Under intense questioning, Danny was reduced to a shell of his former self. The burly driver shrank into his plastic chair and crossed his arms. He stared down at the floor. He was defeated and knew it.

Tyler slid his chair even closer. "We've got your movements on camera, Danny. We have proof you killed Steve, so it's in your best interests to cooperate."

"I wasn't anywhere near the house. I told you, I was waiting outside the dress store." He looked around the room for an escape but there was none.

"Serena told us everything," the Shady Creek detective said. "You planned this whole thing and you're going to spend the rest of your life in prison."

Danny shook his head. "I was waiting in the car the whole time while they were shopping. I can prove it."

The Shady Creek detective stood and walked toward the door. He grabbed the door handle. "We got proof otherwise. You want to give us your version?"

"There is no version. Just the truth," Danny said. "I told you, I wasn't there."

Underneath Danny's tough exterior was a gullible man in love. "There's been some kind of mix-up. Let me talk to her."

"No. Even if we let you, it's a bad idea, Danny." The Shady Creek detective leaned against the wall. "I don't recommend it, especially since she's accusing you of murder."

Danny swore under his breath. His head dropped for a full minute. Then he raised his head and locked eyes with Tyler. "I didn't—he was abusing her, and when she asked for a divorce, he threatened to kill her."

The Shady Creek detective snickered. "This sounds just like a Real McCoy's episode. She's a good actress, I'll give her that. You fell for the drama, didn't you?"

Danny's voice cracked. It's real—I saw the bruises. Serena feared for her life. She begged me to help her."

"She asked you to kill him?" Tyler asked.

"She, uh…didn't actually say those exact words, but I knew what she wanted," Danny said. "I had to help her. If I didn't, we'd never be together."

"You were in love with her." Tyler pushed a box of

tissues on the table closer to Danny. "How long have you been having an affair?"

Danny sighed. "Over a year. She was getting ready to leave him, but then he found out about us. He beat her up, threatened me. He was going to kill us both."

"He confronted you?" Tyler asked.

Danny shook his head. "Not directly. But Serena told me that he had found out about us. She kept saying she would leave, but the show…"

"You just took her word for all of it? She was stringing you along, Danny," The Shady Creek detective said. "She manipulated you to do her dirty work, to kill an innocent man."

"No, no! That's not how it is. She was in danger…we love each other." Danny took a tissue from the box and dabbed his eyes. "She didn't want him dead; she just wanted to leave him, but he wouldn't let her go. I wanted to talk to him alone, to confront him about it all. I went alone, because Serena didn't want me to get involved. That's why I snuck over there while Serena and Abby were out shopping. I wanted to scare him, that's all."

The Shady Creek detective said, "How sweet of you. You're covering for her while she's throwing you under the bus. She's blaming you for everything, Danny. You'll spend the rest of your life in prison; she'll find some new guy."

"No." But for the first time, Danny looked unsure of himself. Judging from his body language, he was genuinely in love with Serena and believed she felt the same.

"You killed him, Danny," Tyler said softly. "With the block of ice you got beforehand. You planned everything. Premeditation is murder-one."

"I never got the ice. It was already there. Serena told me to sneak in through the unlocked front door and get a block of ice from the freezer. I just wanted to scare Steve, rough him up a little." Danny paused. "I barely touched him, and suddenly he was down and out. I panicked and pushed him into the pool."

Serena, at least, had planned Steve's murder. Danny was likely just as guilty, but he was trying to save himself from a first-degree murder charge. As for Jason buying the ice, he was probably an unwitting accomplice. Serena got Jason to buy the items from the store, knowing full well they would be used against his father. Jason also made a convenient scapegoat that could be blamed, but Serena hadn't counted on the other evidence pointing to Danny.

Serena had almost gotten away with the perfect murder, committed by her lover with the evidence pointing to her stepson. Her almost impossibly short timeline would have worked too. If Mom hadn't discovered Steve in the pool, Serena could have delayed discovery of his body, and the death would have surely been labeled an accident.

"She doesn't love you, Danny. Never did. She denies you were ever lovers and claims you acted on your own." Tyler scratched his chin. "

"You're lying!" Danny's eyes flashed with anger. "She was going to leave him for me."

The Shady Creek detective shook his head. "Not according to her. She was planning on firing you. Said you were jealous, had a crush, and that it was awkward. She's already lawyered up and they're going after you, son."

"She never said that," Danny said, desperation in his voice.

CHAPTER 29

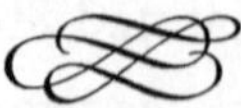

By the time we were ready to drive back to Westwick Corners, the snow had stopped, the roads had been freshly plowed, and the sun had risen on Valentine's Day.

I stifled a yawn as Tyler drove up the windy driveway to the inn. The McCoy's crew had checked out after a rushed breakfast, which was just fine with me. It had been twenty-four hours since I had last slept, and I was in no mood to deal with guests.

My stomach—my now svelte, skinny stomach—craved eggs, toast, and coffee.

Once inside, we made a beeline for the kitchen and loaded our plates with food.

I poured myself a big mug of coffee and headed into the dining room with my breakfast plate. It was laden with scrambled eggs, buttered toast, and a bonus blueberry scone. I had ditched my diet. In the short time since the curse lifted, my body had shrunk back to its pre-curse girth. I suspected that aside from the curse, one of Aunt Pearl's spells had been responsible for my expanded waistline. I'd never be able to prove it though.

Tyler was already seated at one end of the dining room table, an amused expression on his face as he listened to Mom and Aunt Pearl argue back and forth.

"Admit you're wrong and sell the Rocklin place, Ruby."

"I will not! There's no need to, because Cendrine removed the curse."

Tyler frowned. "What is this curse that everyone keeps talking about?"

Aunt Pearl held a finger to her lips. "Sshh! Just mentioning it gives us bad luck."

Mom laughed. "Mention it all you want because it's not real. However, a good curse story is exactly the thing that attracts tourists. I'm glad Cen worked her magic, but I never, ever believed in the Rocklin curse. It's just a myth."

My thoughts drifted as I sipped my coffee. Everything was good again. It was Valentine's Day, Tyler and I had plans for dinner at a fancy restaurant tonight, and he was going to—wait! How could he propose with a missing engagement ring?

Tyler stood and walked over to the window. "Can we postpone our dinner, Cen? The roads are icy, and I don't feel like driving all the way back to Shady Creek again. I'd rather stay here."

Was it because of the snow or just an excuse for a lost ring?

"Sure." I was both relieved and disappointed. At least it

gave me a chance to deal with Aunt Pearl and the missing ring.

"We'll go another time. Tonight, I'd like to make you a special Valentine's Day dinner instead."

"Well, that's a first!" Aunt Pearl said sarcastically.

"Matter of fact, why don't I cook us all dinner?" Tyler smiled.

And he did.

CHAPTER 30

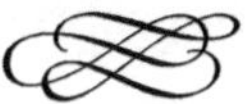

With the curse gone, I was able to wear my beautiful beaded dress. It was even more gorgeous than I remembered, and it easily zipped up. I stood in front of my bedroom full-length mirror, pleased, and also a little relieved, that it fit. If anything, it was even a tiny bit loose.

I took one last look and then headed downstairs into the dining room where the table was set with Mom's best china. There was Caesar salad, freshly baked garlic bread, and several steaming hot vegetable dishes.

Tyler emerged from the kitchen carrying a dish of baked chicken fettucine. He placed the dish on the table and came over to the foot of the stairs. He took me in his arms and kissed me. "Cen, you look beautiful."

I gazed at my handsome boyfriend with his irresistible smile, thinking how incredibly lucky I was.

Mom entered the dining room with a large casserole dish, and Aunt Pearl trailed behind her, empty-handed.

Mom smiled at Tyler as she placed the casserole dish on the table. "You never said you could cook."

"I'm not a gourmet like you, Ruby. Your talent is truly magical."

"Smartass." Aunt Pearl grabbed a slice of garlic bread from the plate on the table and took a bite.

"You do seem to like my cooking," Tyler said.

I was amazed. "Where did you find the time to do all this? When did you have time to shop?"

Tyler smiled. "I always plan ahead."

There was a knock at the front door, Mom answered, and returned a minute later with Aunt Pearl's boyfriend, Earl. He took a seat beside Aunt Pearl, opposite from Tyler and me. Mom sat at the head of the table and Grandma Vi floated above the empty chair at the foot of the table, humming a song.

This was going to be fun.

It was a family dinner instead of a romantic one. Or maybe it would be a little bit of both. Romantic love, family love, it's all good. Tyler was practically a member of the family now, and it was time to tell him about by ghostly grandma. There was a time and place for everything, but this wasn't quite the right time.

Something was about to happen.

Earl stood and walked into the living room. Seconds later, he returned with a guitar. He slung the strap over his shoulder and walked toward the table. He stopped beside Aunt Pearl and began to strum.

"Earl? What is going on?" Aunt Pearl's face flushed, and

her eyes widened.

Earl smiled, his fingers deftly working the strings as he sang:

Love is in the air,
  Love is in the air,

I was not aware,
  How much I cared,
  Until love was in the air,

I did not see,
  How much you cared for me,
  Until love was in the air,

Love is in the air,
  Love is in the air,

A feeling beyond compare,
  Will you wait for me?

I breathe you in,
  Your heart I will win,
  Now that love is in the air,

. . .

I'LL HOLD YOU DEAR,
  Whenever you are near,
  Now that love is in the air,

LOVE IS IN THE AIR,
  Love is in the air,

OUR SECRET AFFAIR,
  For all to see,
  With Love in the air,

MY HEART STILL BEATS,
  Whenever we meet,
  Now that love is in the air,

I BREATHE IN DEEP,
  And promise to keep,
  Our hearts so deep,
  In this love affair,

I TAKE YOUR HAND,
  Let me be your man,
  Now that love is in the air.

AUNT PEARL BLUSHED. "OH, EARL, STOP."

"It's so beautiful, Earl." Mom clasped her hands together, misty-eyed. "Did you write it yourself?"

Earl glanced at Aunt Pearl before answering. "It's a song I set to music."

I clapped. "I didn't know you wrote songs, Earl. It's very beautiful. You're as talented a songwriter as you are a musician."

"I uh…didn't write the words. Pearl did. I just set them to music."

"Pearl wrote a love song?" Mom's eyes widened. "I-I don't believe it!"

Aunt Pearl said, "It's not a love song, Ruby. I just rhymed some words. I don't see why it's such a big deal."

Mom laughed. "It is a huge deal, Pearl. It's oh so…uh, romantic."

"Why is that funny? It's just a stupid song." Aunt Pearl jumped from her chair. "You weren't supposed to tell anyone, Earl."

"Well, I guess the secret's out now." Earl placed a hand gently on Aunt Pearl's arm. "Don't be mad, Pearl."

Pearl opened her mouth but didn't say anything. She looked stunned. "I'll get dessert."

I laughed. "But we haven't even eaten dinner yet!"

Aunt Pearl glared at me before beating a hasty retreat into the kitchen.

Was Aunt Pearl embarrassed at Earl's proposal, or was it the fact that he did it in front of all of us?

"You two seriously thought you were keeping things secret?" Tyler laughed. "We all knew this was coming."

Earl shrugged. "Pearl's the one who wanted it that way.

She said it would ruin her reputation. But I say that pretending just keeps you from true happiness."

Earl was the only person in the world who could defy Aunt Pearl and get away with it.

He winked. "She can run but she can't hide. I had to propose in front of everyone, just so she won't pretend it didn't happen. With a little luck and coercion, I think she'll come around to my way of thinking."

The kitchen door flew open and Aunt Pearl emerged with Mom's chocolate ganache cake. She placed it in the center of the table and sat down, avoiding eye contact with everyone at the table, including Earl.

He turned to her. "Pearl will you…."

Her hand flew to her mouth. "Not here, Earl."

He ignored her. He sang, *"Pearl will you please…"*

She waved her hand in protest, but the corners of her mouth turned up into a smile. "Stop before you embarrass yourself. Everybody, help yourself to cake."

Earl strummed a few chords on his guitar, a faster, upbeat tempo this time:

"Pearl, oh Pearl,
You're the gal for me,
Do me a favor,
And spend your days with me.
Will you, Pearl?
Say you will—"

.   .   .

AUNT PEARL'S face was so red it almost matched her red velour jumpsuit. "Will I what?"

Earl winked. "You know what I'm asking, Pearl." He began to strum his guitar again, his voice rising from a low whisper:

"REVEAL OUR SECRET AFFAIR,
Without nary a care,
Now that love is in the air."

EARL PAUSED and waited for an answer.

The room was completely silent.

"Oh Earl, will you please stop?"

Earl, ever persistent, resumed playing:

"WILL YOU SAY YES,
Don't make me guess,
Now that love—"

"OKAY, okay, fine. You won't take no for an answer so fine, have it your way. Yes, I'll do it! Now will you please stop?" Aunt Pearl flicked her wrist at Earl as if to shoo him and his guitar away.

Mom's hand flew to her mouth. "Is this what I think it is?"

Earl smiled. "Whatever it is you're thinking, Ruby, you're probably right."

"Earl, please!" Aunt Pearl looked around the table, clearly mortified at the marriage proposal that had unfolded in front of all of us. She scanned our faces to gauge our reactions before lowering her gaze to her plate.

Earl looked crestfallen. He bit his lip, clearly not expecting Aunt Pearl's reaction.

Everyone in the room knew that Earl's song was a proposal in disguise.

That included Aunt Pearl.

Was she so oblivious to Earl's hurt feelings?

"After a moment, she said, "Geesh, okay, Earl. Just put that darn guitar away and eat your dinner."

Earl broke into a broad smile as he stood and removed his guitar. He walked over to the wall and leaned the guitar against it, then returned to the table and sat down. "You know I'll do anything for you, Pearl."

"What a sweet man! Don't let this one get away, Pearl!" Mom giggled.

Grandma Vi clasped her hands together. "Bravo!"

Aunt Pearl rolled her eyes. "It's just a song, for crying out loud! Everybody, calm down. I wanted to keep it a secret but that's impossible now. Earl and I decided to try our hand at song writing. I wrote the lyrics and he set it to music. We entered a contest, and we're probably going to win."

Tyler grinned. "Oh really? Where can I find out more about this contest?"

Aunt Pearl smirked at Tyler. "You can't. I doubt you could write a good song, but even if you did, it's too late. The deadline was a week ago."

Maybe they really had composed a song, and maybe

there was a real contest, but I doubted it. I couldn't imagine Aunt Pearl writing romantic lyrics, much less making them public for a song contest.

Earl had just proposed, and Aunt Pearl had accepted in her own strange way. One thing was certain: she wouldn't have reacted well to Earl getting down on one knee and popping the question. Earl was both subtle and yet public, with his cryptic way of announcing their love to the world —or at least to our family. That was something that Aunt Pearl could never do herself. She would never admit to being in love with Earl or wanting to marry him. In his own sweet way, he understood her like no one else did. His carefully crafted proposal allowed Aunt Pearl to save face and keep her grumpy image. Yet Earl also got the upper hand with his cheeky proposal.

THIRTY MINUTES LATER, we sat around the dining room table, stuffed after a delicious dinner. Mom and I made plans for an extravagant wedding for Earl and Aunt Pearl. Earl played some more songs on his guitar while Tyler cut and served slices of Mom's chocolate ganache cake.

Mom's baking always amazed me. Every creation seemed sprinkled with magic, though I knew that she always baked from scratch without any witchcraft whatsoever. That required a lot of willpower because witches can conjure up pretty much anything. But baking, like life in general, has no real shortcuts. You get out exactly what you put into it, no more and no less.

As I savored the rich chocolate, my tooth bit down on

something hard. I placed the napkin to my lips and spit out the offending rock.

I opened the napkin to find a cake-encrusted ring.

A beautiful solitaire engagement ring.

It was identical to the ring Aunt Pearl had pulled out of Tyler's jacket pocket, except for one detail. This ring was a pink diamond solitaire, not a white diamond solitaire. But —Earl had just serenaded Aunt Pearl with a marriage proposal. This ring couldn't possibly be for me. "Oh no! Aunt Pearl I think I got—"

"Thank goodness. I really thought you were going to eat that thing!" Mom exclaimed.

The beautiful pink gemstone gleamed as light reflected off the facets. Tyler really had bought a ring, only it was a different ring than the one that Aunt Pearl had taunted me with earlier. Hers was a copycat ring with one big difference: her conjured-up ring had a white diamond instead of a pink diamond like the one before me now. Aunt Pearl had missed one important detail when casting her mischievous spell. None of that mattered now.

Tyler pushed back his chair and got down on one knee. "Cendrine West, will you marry me?"

ALSO BY COLLEEN CROSS

Westwick Witches Cozy Mysteries

Witch You Well

Rags to Witches

Witch and Famous

Christmas Witch List

Witching Hour Dead

Witching for Love on Valentines Day

Katerina Carter Fraud Legal Thrillers

Exit Strategy

Game Theory

Blowout

Greenwash

Red Handed

Blue Moon

Nonfiction

Anatomy of a Ponzi Scheme